ATTACK OF
THE JACK

Goosebumps®™

Goosebumps® MOST WANTED™

Scholastic Children's Books
An imprint of Scholastic Ltd
Euston House, 24 Eversholt Street, London, NW1 1DB, UK
Registered office: Westfield Road, Southam, Warwickshire, CV47 0RA
SCHOLASTIC, GOOSEBUMPS, GOOSEBUMPS HORRORLAND and
associated logos are trademarks and/or registered trademarks of Scholastic Inc.

First Published in the US by Scholastic Inc, 2017
First published in the UK by Scholastic Ltd, 2019

Copyright © Scholastic Inc, 2017

ISBN 978 1407 19574 2

Goosebumps books created by Parachute Press, Inc.
A CIP catalogue record for this book
is available from the British Library.

Printed by CPI Group (UK) Ltd, Croydon, CR0 4YY
Papers used by Scholastic Children's Books are made
from wood grown in sustainable forests.

3 5 7 9 10 8 6 4 2

www.scholastic.co.uk

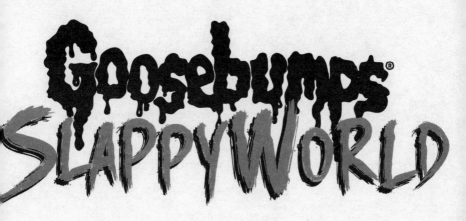

ATTACK OF THE JACK

R.L. STINE

■ SCHOLASTIC

SLAPPY HERE, EVERYONE.

Welcome to *SlappyWorld*.

Yes, it's Slappy's world—you're only *screaming* in it! Hahaha.

Readers Beware: Don't call me a dummy, Dummy. I'm so bright, you need to wear sunglasses when I come into a room. Haha.

Know why I was the smartest one in my class? Because I was the ONLY one in my class! Hahaha!

Do you know the only one who is smarter than me? ME! Hahaha!

I know that doesn't make any sense. But you don't want to be the one to tell me that—*do* you, slave?

I'm smart and I'm generous, too. I'm such a nice guy. Know what I like to share? Horrifying stories to make you scream and shake. Ha.

I don't want to keep you up all night. I want to keep you up FOREVER! Hahaha.

Take this story. It's about a sister and brother named Violet and Shawn. They don't know it,

1

but they are about to go on the most terrifying sailing trip ever.

I don't want to spoil the story, but here's a hint: Their ship isn't exactly waterproof!

Hope you don't get seasick, slave! Hahaha.

Go ahead. Start the story. I call it *Attack of the Jack!*

It's just one more tale from *SlappyWorld*!

2

I sat on the edge of the seat and pressed my nose against the window as our bus bumped over the narrow road. A wooden sign came into view. It had a black ship's anchor across the top above the words: *Welcome to Sea Urchin Cove.*

"We're here," I told my brother, Shawn.

He didn't look up from the *Battle Soccer* game on his phone. "I can smell the ocean," he said.

I pushed up the bus window. Yes, I smelled it, too. The air felt heavy and damp and smelled like fish and salt.

My name is Violet Packer. I'm twelve, two years older than Shawn. Shawn and I had been to the ocean only once, five years ago on a family vacation.

I was seven and he was five. It rained every day, and we never got to swim or even play on the beach.

Now, here we were in this little New England seaside village, about to meet our uncle Jim for the first time. Mom and Dad had to travel for work this summer. They thought this would be a great vacation for us. We'd spend our time with Uncle Jim and fish and sail and do whatever people who live near the ocean like to do. A whole new world for Shawn and me.

The bus slowed to a halt at the end of a row of low wooden buildings. Across the way, I saw a man with a thick black beard walking quickly along the storefronts. He had a heavy-looking fisherman's net rolled up on his shoulders. Two young women in shorts and sleeveless T-shirts stepped out of a small hotel named *The Sail Inn*.

I bumped Shawn with my shoulder. "Put the game away. We're here," I said again. "Check out this cool village."

Shawn removed his earbuds and slid the phone into his shorts pocket. He's not like most little brothers. Shawn is very obedient. Mom said I was in charge this summer and, so far, Shawn had taken it seriously.

He isn't a pest like a lot of brothers. He doesn't tease me or try to start arguments or act like some kind of brat.

He pretty much kept to himself during the long bus ride from Yellow Springs. He read his baseball books and played sports games on his phone.

The only time he got really excited and turned

to stare out the window was when four cows started chasing the bus somewhere in upstate New York.

I think Shawn and I get along so much better than most sisters and brothers because we're very different from each other.

He isn't shy. But he likes to spend time by himself.

I like to talk and gossip and sing and laugh with my friends. I like a good joke and everyone tells me I'm pretty funny. I get really excited about things, like this trip to Sea Urchin Cove to meet Uncle Jim.

And I'm definitely not into sports, like Shawn. I don't spend all my time watching ESPN and reading baseball novels and playing in Little League every weekend.

I'm tall and thin and I've been taking ballet lessons since I was six, and I love it, and my teachers say I'm a very promising dancer. Of course, I live in Yellow Springs, Ohio, not New York City, where the great ballet schools are located. But Mom says if I'm still so devoted when I'm in high school, she'll take me to New York for auditions.

But right now I was in Sea Urchin Cove, and that was pretty exciting, too.

There were only six people on the bus. And Shawn and I were the only ones getting off here. The driver pulled down our suitcases for us and carried them to the sidewalk, which was made of wooden planks.

As the bus rumbled away, I shielded my eyes from the sun with one hand and searched for Uncle Jim. But there was no one waiting for us.

"Mom warned us that Jim is absent-minded," I reminded Shawn.

Shawn frowned. "Does that mean he doesn't remember we are coming today?"

"No. It just means he's late," I said.

Seagulls squawked loudly, flapping over the flat roofs of the low storefronts. In a wide space between a hardware store and a bait store, I could see water. Dark green waves shimmered in the sunlight. A small boat bobbed at a dock, and men were unloading silvery fish onto a wooden cart.

"This looks like a movie set," Shawn said.

"Yeah. *Jaws*, maybe," I joked. I hummed some shark-attack theme music.

He laughed. "Hey, Violet, I'm hungry."

"Me too," I said. "Why don't we go get some lunch while we wait for Uncle Jim to show up?"

Carrying our suitcases with us, we found a little restaurant at the end of the block. It looked like a wooden shack. A sign in the window read: THE WHISTLING CLAM.

"Remember those clam rolls we had when we went to the ocean that summer?" I said.

Shawn shook his head. "No. I was too young. All I remember is it rained every day, and we had to stay in our cottage and play Monopoly with Mom and Dad."

I glanced up at the sky. Bright blue. Not a cloud.

We dragged our bags into the little restaurant and had clam rolls and French fries for lunch. There were only four tables in the place. Three men sat at the counter, eating silently.

The waitress was very nice. The nametag on her uniform shirt said MARIANNE. She brought us extra coleslaw and Cokes and said it was on the house.

She lingered at the side of our table while we ate. "Where are you two from?" she asked. She had a smoky, hoarse voice.

I told her Yellow Springs, Ohio. "Going to stay with my uncle," I said.

She wiped at a stain on her apron. "Who's your uncle?"

"His name is Jim Finnegan," I said.

She gasped.

Her mouth dropped open.

"Admiral Jim?" Her voice was suddenly tiny.

I nodded yes, and she took a step back. Her eyes were still wide with surprise.

"What's wrong?" I asked.

"You don't want to stay with Admiral Jim,"

she said, and her voice trembled. "You need to make other plans. Or . . . take the first bus back to Yellow Springs."

Shawn pushed his plate away. He had gone very pale.

"I—I don't understand," I stammered.

"Listen to me," Marianne said, grabbing my shoulder. "Don't stay in that falling-down old lighthouse with that crazy old coot. I'm warning you."

Shawn and I just stared at her. I felt a shock of dread tightening my stomach. I took a deep breath. "This is the part where you say you're joking," I said.

"Right. Please say you were just messing with us," Shawn added.

She shook her head, her lips tight, eyes still wide. "I'm not joking, kids. Believe me. No one in Sea Urchin Cove wants to go near your uncle. Admiral Jim is hiding something in that old lighthouse. Something evil."

2

Shawn and I ended up walking to Uncle Jim's lighthouse. The whole village was only two blocks long. A small open-air market stood at the end.

Then the land sloped slowly down, covered in tall green reeds. The reeds swayed one way, then the other, blown by the gusting bursts of wind off the ocean.

We could see the tall gray lighthouse perched on a low rocky cliff at the edge of the ocean. White-capped waves splashed against the shore from the shimmering blue-green waters.

Dragging our heavy suitcases at our sides, we followed a narrow, sandy path that curved gently through the field of tall reeds. Insects buzzed in the reeds, and I saw two dark eyes that turned out to belong to a rabbit peering at us.

Shawn didn't talk for a long time. He appeared lost in thought. Finally, he stepped beside me on the path. "You don't think that waitress was serious, do you, Violet?"

"Of course not," I replied. "Mom and Dad said that Uncle Jim is a little strange because he's lived alone for so long. They said he's absent-minded and weird about some things. But, remember? They said he is a lot of fun."

Shawn nodded. "Yeah, I remember. They said he had a million good stories."

"And they didn't say he's evil," I said, jumping over a small pile of stones in the sand. "They would *never* have sent us here if he was evil or hiding something evil in his lighthouse."

"Of course not," Shawn murmured.

The sun was beginning to burn the back of my neck. I set down my suitcase and rubbed my neck with one hand. Then I swept my light brown hair off my perspiring forehead with both hands.

Shawn's eyes grew wide and he pointed behind me. "Hey—look what's following us."

Blinking into the sun, I lowered my gaze and saw it. A large black cat. It had green eyes trained on us. Its tail was arched behind it.

I turned toward it and knelt down. "Hey, kitten," I said softly, "are you following us?"

The cat tilted its head as if trying to understand. The green eyes stared up at me without blinking.

"Are you bad luck?" Shawn asked it. "Is it true what they say about black cats?"

The cat whipped around suddenly and vanished into the reeds.

I laughed. "Shawn, you insulted it."

A few minutes later, we came to a low brick wall that marked the end of the wide field of reeds. "Check that out," Shawn said, pointing at the wall.

Someone had painted a grinning white skull on the faded bricks. The skull had a big black X over it.

"Not very inviting," I said. "Maybe Uncle Jim *doesn't* like visitors."

"Maybe he did it for a joke," Shawn murmured, staring hard at it.

The lighthouse rose up on the other side of the wall. As we came near, I could see that jagged cracks ran from top to bottom on the sides, and the paint was peeling everywhere.

A gray-shingled house stood a few yards from the lighthouse. The shutters were drawn. A triangle-shaped flag fluttered on a low flagpole in front of the house. The flag was red with a black ship's anchor in its center.

I gazed at the white-capped waves crashing against the shore just beyond the house. A short wooden dock had a tiny boat bobbing at its side. The wind rushed at us off the water.

Shawn's blond hair blew wild around his face. "Let's get out of this wind," he said. "I'm freezing."

I realized I was shivering, too. I don't know if it was because of the wind or because of the creepy, grinning skull.

We helped each other over the low wall. Then we dragged our suitcases to the front door of the little house. It was gray like the shingles, wooden, with the paint peeling. No doorknob.

"Hey, Uncle Jim!" I shouted. But a burst of wind blew my words back into my face.

I leaned forward, trying to dodge the powerful gusts. And the door swung in.

"Uncle Jim?"

No answer.

I lifted my suitcase and stepped inside. I squinted into a cluttered, dimly lit room, the air hot and damp.

Shawn followed me in. And before I could push the door closed, I saw a flurry of motion on the floor. As if blown by the strong wind, the black cat darted into the house.

"Hey—" I called after it.

But the cat leaped to the center of the room, onto a dark, round throw rug. It sat on its haunches and gazed around slowly, its green eyes wide and unblinking.

Then, in a hoarse, scratchy voice, the cat said, "Admiral Jim! Visitors!"

Shawn and I stared at the cat with our mouths open. Then we turned to each other with the same question on our faces: *Did we just hear that?*

The black cat tilted its head as if waiting for an answer. Then it repeated, "Admiral Jim?"

I heard someone groan. And then a loud squeaking sound.

I turned to the doorway to our left. It led to another room. And in the doorway, I could see a large man slowly sit up from a white rope hammock.

With another groan, he dropped his feet to the floor. Sweeping back his long white hair, he lumbered to his feet. He wore a white sailor uniform. His big belly bulged out from under the shirt.

He had a round, red face—cherry red—and kept blinking his large blue eyes. His thick mustache was as white as his hair. He pulled on a white admiral's cap as he walked unsteadily toward us.

He stretched and yawned and then squinted, first at Shawn, then at me. "My niece and nephew, have ye arrived?" he said in a booming voice that seemed to rumble up from deep in his chest. "I apologize. I wasn't expecting ye till later."

The cat tsk-tsked.

"Uncle Jim?" I suddenly couldn't speak. He was so huge and red-faced and old. His uniform was wrinkled, and a big stretch of his stomach showed through his open shirt buttons.

"Welcome! Welcome!" He threw his arms up and dove forward to wrap us both in a hug. "So sorry I wasn't there to greet you. The cat was supposed to wake me."

"Do tell," the cat muttered, shaking its head.

"The cat—it talks?" I finally found my voice.

Shawn took a step back. I think this was all too weird for him.

Uncle Jim nodded. "Yes, she does." He leaned toward the cat. "Tell our visitors your name."

"Celessste," the cat hissed, her pink tongue licking her front teeth.

A grin stretched over our uncle's face, making his mustache spread like two wings. "Forgive her slight lisp."

"But—that's impossible!" Shawn cried.

Uncle Jim kept his eyes on the cat. "Do you think it's impossible, Celeste?"

"No," the cat immediately replied.

14

"It's some kind of a trick," Shawn insisted. "The cat is a robot, right? A robot with artificial intelligence?"

Uncle Jim tilted back his admiral's cap and scratched his white hair. "I don't know what that means, young Shawn." He petted Celeste's back. "A cat is a cat, I think."

He picked up our suitcases. "Follow me. Let's get ye settled. Then I'll tell ye the story of my cat."

I'd been so startled by seeing him and the cat, I hadn't looked at the front room at all. As Shawn and I followed our uncle to a narrow stairway against the back wall, it all started to come into focus.

He had a huge fisherman's net draped over one wall. The net was filled with dozens of seashells, crab and lobster shells, and dozens of starfish.

The room was so cluttered with objects, there was little space to walk. I saw a black cannon with four cannonballs stacked in front of it. A ship's anchor leaning against a skull-and-crossbones pirate flag. Two big wooden chests with carvings of mermaids on the sides. Shelves of toys and knickknacks and colored bottles and tiny model ships.

"This is awesome," I whispered to Shawn.

Shawn nodded. "Like being in a weird museum."

Uncle Jim stopped at the bottom of a steep,

narrow staircase. "Ye'll be sleeping in the crow's nest," he boomed. "Careful. The old wooden stairs are a bit rickety."

I peered up toward the top of the stairs. Shadowy gray light washed over a bare wall.

A suitcase in each hand, Uncle Jim squeezed into the stairway. He started up the stairs, but then turned back to us.

"Don't worry," he said. "The ghost seldom comes out in the daytime."

Shawn and I exchanged glances. *Was he serious?*

We found two tiny rooms upstairs. The crow's nest, as our uncle called it. Each room had a small dresser with a lamp on top, and a rope hammock strung between wooden posts.

Uncle Jim set down the suitcases. "I'll bet ye've never slept in a hammock before," he said, smiling again, making his mustache flutter.

Shawn squeezed a hand over the ropes, testing it. "Do people really sleep in these things?"

That made Jim laugh. "Ye'll sleep like a baby seal."

Do baby seals sleep a lot? I wondered.

I unpacked some of the clothes from my suitcase and stuffed them into the small dresser. The rest I left in the suitcase. I shoved the suitcase against one wall.

Then I hurried down the narrow, creaking stairway to rejoin Uncle Jim. I couldn't wait to hear more about the cat.

I found Uncle Jim sitting across from Shawn at a tiny wooden table in a corner of the kitchen.

Bursts of wind off the ocean rattled the kitchen window. Over the rush of the wind, I could hear waves crashing hard on the shore.

Celeste hadn't moved from the round rug in the center of the front room. She was curled up tightly, making soft purring sounds as she slept.

Had I imagined her talking?

No. I definitely had heard her speak.

I sat down across from Uncle Jim. He pushed a tall brown mug across the table to me. "Ye must be thirsty after your journey, Violet," he said. "Some sailors' grog will refresh you."

I gazed into the mug. "Sailors' grog?"

"Actually, it's Diet Sprite," he said. "The village store doesn't carry real grog."

Outside the window, I could see part of the lighthouse, solid and gray, throwing its shadow over the house.

"Have ye heard from your parents?" Jim asked. He rubbed his mustache. "Three weeks in Argentina. That's a long business trip. Why didn't they take you with them?"

"They thought we'd have more fun here," I said. "And Mom said it was time Shawn and I met our long-lost uncle."

Jim took a slow drink. "Yes. Ye'll have more fun here. And the food is good, too. Mrs. Henry from the village is bringing us crab cakes and slaw tonight."

Shawn had his eyes on the sleeping cat in the front room. "Celeste," he said. "Does she really talk?"

Jim patted Shawn's arm. "Yes, she does, my lad," he said, lowering his voice to a whisper. "I'll tell ye the story. But I warn ye, it's a sad one."

He took another drink from his mug. I don't think his mug had Diet Sprite. For one thing, it was dark brown.

"Poor Danny Lubbins," Uncle Jim said, rubbing his jaw, his expression suddenly serious. "It's Danny's story, actually, and as I said, it isn't a happy one."

He sighed. "Lost at sea, Danny was," he continued. "One of the best and most loyal sailors I ever met. But the *Spanish Eagle* went down against some rocks. And Danny was lucky to be hurled onto a raft, even though it was only the size of a closet door. And there he was, tossed by the waves, bobbing away from the wreckage of the great old ship."

Uncle Jim shut his eyes, as if picturing the shipwreck. He took a sip from his mug. Behind him, the wind rattled the window.

"Danny huddled with his eyes shut as the rain came down and the waves pitched him this way and that. He knew he didn't have much of a chance on that tiny raft. After a day of tossing in the storm, the clouds parted and the sun came out. Danny opened his eyes—and what do you know? He saw that he wasn't alone."

Jim pointed a finger at the sleeping cat in the next room. "That cat was riding the waves with him. Somehow the ship's cat had made it to the raft. And there it was, staring up at poor Danny . . . poor, superstitious Danny . . . with a black cat his only company in the vast ocean."

Shawn's eyes were wide. "And the two of them survived? They made it to land?" he asked.

Uncle Jim frowned. "Don't get ahead of the story, lad. You see, it's a very long story—because Danny Lubbins was at sea on that tiny slip of a plank raft . . . *for three hundred days*."

Shawn and I both gasped. "Nearly a year," I murmured.

"Just imagine," Jim continued, narrowing his eyes at us. "Under the sun and in terrible storms. With nothing to do but catch fish and eat them raw, and stare into the green eyes of a black cat—for three hundred days."

He paused for a moment. "Poor Danny thought he'd go stark-raving mad. He needed something to think about. The poor lad needed something to do. So long at sea . . . so long at sea . . . He couldn't stand the uncertainty and the silence. Could you?"

Uncle Jim didn't wait for an answer. "So what

did Danny do to keep from going mad? *He taught the cat to talk.*"

I gasped again. Shawn crinkled up his face. In disbelief, I guess.

"Danny needed company," Jim said. "All those hours . . . All those days and days and days. So he taught the cat to talk."

Jim looked from Shawn to me. I think he wanted to see if we believed his story.

I'd never heard of a cat who could learn to talk. But I had to believe his story. I mean, I *heard* the cat talk. I couldn't deny it.

"And then they made it to shore?" Shawn demanded.

Uncle Jim shook his head, lowering his eyes. "Poor Danny. After three hundred days, he spotted land. This very place. A rocky shore but with gentle waves. The cat jumped off the raft and swam to safety. But Danny . . ."

His voice caught in his throat. He coughed. His eyes still stared down at the floor.

"Danny didn't make it. So close he was. So close to a happy ending. But only the cat made it to shore. I found her down the beach from the lighthouse. And I brought her home. But Danny . . ." His voice trailed off again.

"Whoa. Wait a minute, Uncle Jim," I said. "If Danny didn't make it to shore, how do you know the story? How do you know everything that happened?"

"Yes," Shawn agreed instantly. "How do you know all this?"

Jim's blue eyes flashed. "The cat told me, of course. Celeste told me the whole story."

Shawn and I just stared at him.

"There's more," Uncle Jim said, lowering his voice to a whisper. "There's a story everyone in the village believes. About Danny."

He stopped and gazed around. "Some people, you see, say they saw Danny Lubbins—*after* he drowned. They say he came to shore as a ghost. They believe we haven't seen the last of Danny Lubbins. They think . . ."

He took a deep breath. "They think Danny is going to return—because he wants his cat back. They think he will come back here, an angry ghost, and take back what is his."

Shawn and I didn't have time to react. Just as Uncle Jim said those words, the back door swung open.

The door swung open—*and there was no one there.*

5

I screamed. Shawn shoved his chair back, too startled to make a sound.

The wind rushed into the kitchen, cold and salty. It sent a stack of napkins flying into the air and toppled a water glass into the sink.

Uncle Jim jumped to his feet, dove to the door, and, lowering his shoulder, shoved it shut. He turned to us, his face redder than before.

"Got to get the latch on that door fixed," he said. "Don't ye know, that happens all the time. A strong wind just sends the door flying open."

He squinted at us, then laughed. "Did you think that was Danny's ghost? The two of ye got as pale as a schooner sail." That made him laugh even more.

"It startled us, that's all," I said.

"I'm not sure I believe the tales the villagers tell," Jim said, returning to the table. "Anyway, if the ghost of Danny Lubbins returns, he wouldn't use the door—would he?"

Shawn swallowed. A little color was slowly returning to his face. He opened his mouth to say something but stopped.

I followed his gaze. Shawn was watching the cat.

Celeste suddenly raised her head off the rug and sat up. Her black fur stood straight up along her back. She sniffed a few times as her green eyes moved around the room.

Then she tilted her head to one side and said, "Danny?"

"You've heard of Blackbeard the pirate, haven't ye?" Uncle Jim began a new story. "Maybe the most famous pirate of all time."

"I think I've heard the name," I said, trying to remember.

"We're not too into pirates," Shawn confessed. "I saw one of the Johnny Depp pirate movies, but that's about it."

Uncle Jim nodded. "Well, I sailed with one of Blackbeard's great-great-great-grandsons, who was even more famous for a time. Johnny Feathers. That was his name. Because he always wore two white feathers in his cap."

Uncle Jim rubbed his beard. "Johnny said they were valuable ostrich feathers from Madagascar. But they looked like they came off a seagull to me."

He snickered. "I was young but I knew not to

correct Johnny Feathers. He was a good sailor, but he had a temper. He once threw a cook overboard because his roasted chicken was sliced too thin. I know that to be true."

"Wow." I shook my head. "That's tough."

"Kept me on my toes," Jim said. He lifted a cannonball off the floor. He was taking Shawn and me around the house now, showing us some of the many treasures he had collected during all his years at sea.

"Well, what I'm holding here is the cannonball that killed Johnny Feathers."

I stared at it. It was a little smaller than a bowling ball and the same color black. For some reason, I expected to see bloodstains on it. But it was perfectly smooth and clean.

"His men were testing the cannon," Uncle Jim said, balancing the heavy cannonball between both hands. "Johnny walked by at the wrong time. Someone yelled, 'Fire!'

"The ball sent his head sailing into the ocean. Johnny just stood there on the deck for a while. Like he didn't believe his head was gone."

"Were you there? Did you see it?" Shawn whispered.

Jim nodded. "They pulled the cannonball out of the ocean. And they got Johnny's hat back, too, with the feathers still on it."

He shook his head. "But they left Johnny's head at the bottom. The water was so clear that day, we could see Johnny staring up at us from two hundred feet down."

I studied Uncle Jim as he lowered the cannon-ball to the floor. Was he making up these stories? Had they really happened? I couldn't decide.

"How did you get the cannonball?" Shawn asked him.

Jim shrugged. "Just kept it. No one else wanted it. I always was a collector. Never liked to part with anything." He gestured around the room. "As ye can see, I like a lot of souvenirs."

We followed him down a short hall to a back room. The hall had tall bookshelves on both sides. They were filled with books and old-looking toys and games. I saw two model sailing ships in glass bottles. A human skull rested at the top of one shelf.

"And now I'm going to show you my vast treasure," Uncle Jim said. He pulled a chain, and a ceiling light flashed on.

We were in a long, low room without windows. A door with a large, rusted lock on it stood at the back. I gazed in amazement at the clutter of knickknacks and souvenirs. My eyes stopped at two big wooden trunks standing side by side in the center.

"Are those pirate treasure chests?" I asked.

Jim laughed. "They're just treasure chests. I wasn't a pirate, ye know. Sometimes I liked to imagine it, though. Dreamed about being

26

a pirate. But I was just a sailing man. The real pirate days were long before I was born."

He grabbed the lid of one of the chests with both hands and started to push it open. Shawn and I stepped up close. The lid swung up—and we both gasped.

"Gold coins!" I cried. "And jewels! Diamonds! It's filled to the top!"

The contents of the chest sparkled under the ceiling light.

"It really is a pirate treasure chest!" Shawn exclaimed.

Jim held on to the lid. He had a big grin under his white mustache. I think our excitement pleased him.

"I uncovered this chest while leading a voyage to the Fiji Islands," he said. "Can you imagine what I felt when I stumbled upon it buried behind a thick tangle of coconut trees? I thought I was dreaming. I stood there for I-don't-know-how-long. Just staring at what I had found."

I couldn't resist. I dug both hands into the chest and let the gold coins and shimmering jewels run through my fingers.

"This . . . must be worth a million dollars!" Shawn stammered. He watched me run my hands through the treasure, his eyes wide in amazement.

"A million dollars?" Uncle Jim said. "Is that your guess, too, Violet?"

"No way," I said. "It has to be worth at least *ten* million!"

Jim chuckled. "Actually, it's all worthless."

I dropped a handful of coins and stepped back. "Excuse me?"

"It's all fake," Uncle Jim said. "It's counterfeit. Not worth a penny."

"But . . . all this treasure—" I protested.

"The chest was left behind on the island by a movie company," he explained. "They must have been making a pirate film. They didn't even bother to take the chest with them when they finished. The jewels aren't real and neither are the coins."

He sighed as he lowered the lid. "But it's nice to pretend," he said. "All of these treasures I've collected help me remember the wonderful adventures I had on the sea."

He started toward the door. "There's lots for ye to explore here," he said. "I hope ye'll have fun. Feel free to open the chests and explore the shelves and all the closets."

I heard a loud pounding. It seemed to be coming from the back of the house.

"That's Mrs. Henry with our crab cake dinner," Jim said. "I'll go answer the door."

He stopped in the hall and turned around. "Oh. One more thing." He pointed to the door with the big lock on it. "That room back there. That's the only forbidden room. The house is all yours. And you can explore the lighthouse, too. But don't try to go in that room. It's the only room ye must never enter."

He turned and hurried to greet Mrs. Henry.

Shawn and I stayed, gazing around at the awesome collection of souvenirs and treasures and total junk.

My eyes landed on the locked door. What could possibly be in that room? Why would Uncle Jim warn us to keep out?

What was he hiding in that forbidden room?

Shawn and I looked at each other. We didn't say a word. But we were both thinking the same thing.

We knew we couldn't resist. We knew that, as soon as Uncle Jim was out of sight, we would be opening that door.

SLAPPY HERE, EVERYONE . . .

Do you have the feeling this story is about to turn scary?

I suddenly have a creepy-crawly feeling at the back of my neck. Or is that just *termites*? Hahaha.

Shawn and Violet had better get plenty of sleep. The ocean holds many surprises.

Once I held a seashell up to my ear and—guess what? I didn't hear the roar of the ocean. I heard a voice saying, "Slappy, you're the best. Slappy, you're AWESOME."

I was so surprised. It took me a few seconds to realize the voice was ME. I was talking to myself! Hahaha.

Okay, guys—on with the story . . .

I had trouble getting to sleep that night.

I think it was partly because of all the excitement of the day. But it was also because of the howl and whistle of the ocean winds right outside my window.

The sound rose and fell like music. Lying on my back with my eyes shut and the covers pulled up to my chin, I thought I heard high voices singing. And once, when I had almost drifted off to sleep, I thought I heard someone saying my name. *"Violet ... Violet ..."* Whispered on the wind.

I sat straight up and listened. Silence now. And then in another howl of wind against my window, I thought I heard laughter. Shrill, cold laughter.

I shuddered, suddenly chilled from head to foot. I sat there, half-awake with the covers gripped in both hands, squeezing them as if they were some kind of life raft, keeping me afloat. Keeping me afloat like Danny Lubbins.

Why was I thinking of him now?

Was it the soft, chilling voice I heard on the next breath of wind? *"Violet ... Violet ... swimmmmm with meeeeeee."*

"No!" I choked out in a trembling whisper.

I slid onto my back and pulled the blanket over my head. I pushed my head deep into the pillow. I had to drown out the voices. I had to shut out the laughing wail of the wind.

When I awoke, the red morning sun was a big ball outside my window, and the wind had calmed. Seagulls cawed loudly outside the window.

I started to lower my feet to the floor—and saw Celeste curled up at the foot of my bed.

She raised her head, blinked her green eyes, and said in her scratchy cat voice, "Good morning. Did you have a nightmare?"

I blinked myself fully awake. I squinted at the cat, at her pale green eyes gazing into mine.

I still couldn't get used to the idea of a cat talking. Her words sent a shiver to the back of my neck. But I said good morning back.

I pulled on a pair of red shorts and an oversized white T-shirt, brushed out my hair, and hurried down the narrow, rickety staircase to the kitchen. Shawn was already at the table, and Uncle Jim was serving him a big omelet.

"Good morning, Violet," Jim said, motioning with his head for me to take my place at the table. His long white hair was unbrushed and fell in tangles at the sides of his red face. He had a gray sweatshirt pulled down over baggy white pants.

"Lobster omelet on the menu this morning," he said in his booming, deep voice. "And sourdough toast. Aren't we the fancy ones? Bet ye don't get this at home."

"We usually have Froot Loops," Shawn said.

Jim chuckled. "Did ye sleep well, Violet?" he asked, scooping some of the eggs onto my plate.

"Not really," I confessed. "The wind . . . I kept hearing all these voices in the wind. It kind of creeped me out."

He scooped the remaining eggs onto his plate and set the pan down. "There *are* voices in the wind," he said. "The voices of all the poor sailors who never made it to shore. They're still alive, Violet. Their bodies are at the bottom of the sea. But their voices live on, carried by the wind."

He narrowed his eyes at me. "I'm surprised you heard them on your first night here. Maybe you have a gift. Maybe you have a talent for hearing things most people can't hear."

I shuddered. "Stop it, Uncle Jim. You're scaring me."

Shawn had a speck of egg on his chin. I wiped it off for him. "I looked outside this morning," he said. "The waves are really high."

"I plan to take you sailing," Jim said. "But today is not the day. The ocean is growling today. That's an old sailor saying. My little boat was nearly tossed out of the water this morning."

I swallowed a chunk of lobster. We never had lobster back home in Ohio. It was chewy and delicious.

Celeste came striding into the kitchen with her tail straight up.

34

"I think you made a friend in Celeste," Uncle Jim said to me. "I saw her heading up to your room last night."

"I was so surprised to see her in my bed when I woke up," I replied.

Celeste tilted her head at my uncle. "Admiral Jim, breakfast, pleasssse."

He scooped a chunk of omelet from his plate into the cat's bowl, and she hungrily lowered her head to it.

"You should put Celeste on TV," Shawn said. "Or do some videos. They would go viral instantly."

Jim rubbed his mustache. "Viral? Like a disease?"

"Shawn means Celeste could be popular," I said. "A star. She's a talking cat! She could make you rich!"

"I think Celeste deserves a quiet life," Jim said, eyeing the cat as she finished her omelet and licked the bowl. "After three hundred days at sea, I don't think she craves any more excitement. As for treasure, my memories are my treasures now."

The cat raised her eyes to Uncle Jim. "More?" she said.

He laughed. "Celeste, you'll never be a star if you get fat."

He filled our glasses with cranberry juice. "I have to do some work on the lighthouse this morning," he said. "The lantern is in need of serious cleaning."

He glanced out the window. "You two could wander down to the beach, if ye like. But be careful. The tide is in and the waves are high, and the rocks down to the sand can be very slippery."

Shawn and I exchanged glances. "I think we want to stay in and explore more of the house," I said. Again, I knew we were both thinking about that locked room.

"Good idea," Uncle Jim said. He drank his juice down in one gulp. "I should be back by lunchtime. Then maybe I'll take ye down and introduce ye to the water."

Why were Shawn and I so drawn to that forbidden room? There was so much to see in our uncle's house. It would take *days* to examine every shelf and collection and treasure chest. So many wonders to explore.

But we were both drawn to that locked room as if it pulled us like a powerful magnet. We watched Uncle Jim stride along the narrow, sandy path that led to the entrance of the lighthouse next door. We saw him pull open the wooden door and disappear inside.

And then, without another word, Shawn and I hurried down the hall to the back room. I pulled the chain and the ceiling light flashed on.

My eyes swept over the two treasure chests in the middle of the room, the shelves of souvenirs and weird objects on the walls. My heart began to pound a little faster as my eyes stopped at the rusted lock on the door of the forbidden room.

"Hey—check this out!" Shawn held up a round, greenish object he had taken off a shelf. I took a few steps closer.

"Is this a real shrunken head?" Shawn said. He held it by the hair and waved it at me. It was about the size of a grapefruit.

"Ohh, gross," I said. "Put it down. Yes, it looks like a real human head."

"All shriveled," Shawn said. "But it still has its eyes. Where do you think Uncle Jim got it?"

"Put it down," I insisted. "I'm sure he has a totally creepy story he'll tell us about whose head it is and how he got it."

"Cool," Shawn said. He lowered the head to the shelf.

Shawn followed me across the room. We both stared at the old lock on the door against the back wall.

"Are we going to do this or not?" I asked.

"We *have* to," Shawn said. "I hate mysteries and so do you. We have to know what's hiding in there."

"We have one problem," I said. "We have to find the key."

Shawn scratched his head. "It could be any-where. It could be hidden in this room. Or anywhere in the house. How could we ever find it?"

I wrapped my hand around the lock. It was so rusty, it scratched my palm.

I gave it a sharp tug—and the lock fell apart.

Startled, I jumped back. The old lock just crumbled in my hand.

I tugged it off the door. Shawn and I stared for a long moment at the rusted doorknob. Then I took a deep breath. "Let's do this," I said.

I grabbed the knob, twisted it, pulled open the door—and gasped.

Pale light poured into the room from behind Shawn and me. Gripping the knob in one hand, I leaned into the doorway, shocked by what I was staring at.

The room was bare.

No furniture. No tall shelves bursting with knickknacks and souvenirs. The room had no windows. The floor was empty, too.

I pulled the door open all the way, letting more light in. Shawn stood beside me, shaking his head. "This is the forbidden room? There's nothing here. Is this one of Uncle Jim's jokes?"

Then, in deep shadow, something came into focus against the back wall. I took a few steps into the room. I spotted a light switch and clicked on a dim ceiling light.

In the light, I could see the whole room clearly. The walls were concrete stones from floor to ceiling. Against the back wall, the dark shape I had spotted turned out to be a tall chest.

I pointed. "It's like the treasure chests in the other room." My voice sounded hollow in the small stone room.

Our shoes scraped on the concrete floor as we stepped up to the chest. The wooden chest was painted black. But it looked gray under a thick layer of dust. A heavy chain was wrapped tightly around it, and a rusted lock, much like the one on the door, hung from the lid.

"Maybe this chest has *real* pirate treasure in it," I said. "Maybe it's worth millions of dollars. And Uncle Jim keeps it locked and chained to make sure it's safe."

"Then we *definitely* have to open it," Shawn said.

"What if there is a pirate curse on it?" I said. "Don't the pirates put curses on things in the Johnny Depp movies?"

Shawn laughed. "You're starting to sound like Uncle Jim. Since when do you believe in evil curses?"

I shrugged.

Shawn grabbed the lock. "I'll bet this is like the lock on the door. Watch it crumble to pieces with one tug."

He gave it a hard tug. The chain bounced against the lid. But the lock didn't fall apart. He jerked it again, twisting the lock against the chain. He tried one more time, pulling with all his strength.

"This one isn't cooperating," I said. "Let's try the chain. Maybe there's a weak link."

I grabbed the chain. It was heavier than I thought. The metal was scratchy from rust. But no matter how much I tugged it and twisted it, I couldn't get it to break apart.

"I think Uncle Jim really wants to keep this one a secret," I said, wiping sweat off my forehead with the back of my hand.

"There has to be a key to the lock," Shawn said, staring at it. He rubbed his jaw. "Now where would Uncle Jim hide the key?"

I gazed around the empty stone room. "Nowhere here to hide it," I decided. "I'll bet he keeps the key on him. You know. Maybe on a chain around his neck. To make sure no one can find it."

I suddenly realized that Shawn wasn't listening to me. He was walking along the wall, rubbing a hand on the stones.

"Shawn, what are you doing?" I demanded.

He didn't answer. He stopped. He tapped a stone on the wall just above his head. "Look, Violet. This stone. It's lighter than the others. It's a different color."

"So?" I said. "Why are we interested in the stones?"

"I'll show you," he said. He curled his hand and began clawing at the stone. I saw that he was trying to press his fingernails into the cracks between the stone and the rest of the wall.

It took a minute or so to manage it. Then he wiggled the stone right out of the wall. "I knew it!" he cried. He reached into the hole—and pulled out a large brass key.

I clapped my hands. "Shawn, when did you become a genius?" I said.

"When I was born," he said, grinning, showing off the two deep dimples in his cheeks.

He handed me the key. I held my breath and lowered it to the rusted lock. It slid in easily. I gave it a turn and the lock popped open.

"This is almost *too* easy," I said. I turned to my brother. "Last chance to forget about this room, forget this trunk, and go find somewhere else to explore."

Shawn tugged at the heavy steel chain. "No way. It's too late to chicken out, Violet. We've already undone the lock."

I let out a sigh. "Okay. Here we go."

I tugged the chain off the trunk and let it clatter to the floor. Then Shawn and I both grabbed the latch and clicked it open.

I reached for the lid of the chest, preparing to push it open. But I stopped when I heard a sound behind us at the doorway.

Shawn and I both turned to the sound. My heart skipped a beat when I saw Celeste sitting upright inside the door.

The cat's green eyes slid from Shawn to me. Her tail waved once, moving silently over the concrete floor.

Then Celeste tilted her head to one side and said, "I'm telling Admiral Jim."

"No—wait!" I cried. "Please—"

But before I could move, the cat whirled around and disappeared, her tail held straight behind her.

"Celeste—please!" Shawn shouted. He jumped to his feet and ran to the door. A second later, he turned back to me. "She's gone."

He walked back to the chest, shaking his head. "Who knew the cat was a snitch?" he murmured.

He dropped down beside me. I was still on my knees, ready to push open the chest lid. "Now what?" Shawn asked. "We're busted. We're in major trouble, I guess."

"Then we might as well go ahead and open this chest," I replied. "I mean, if we're already in trouble, what difference will it make?"

Shawn nodded. "This better be good," he said.

We both gripped the lid and pushed it up. It took a few tries. The lid was stuck. We both groaned as we pushed the thing up with all our strength.

It made a popping sound as it finally came loose—and we swung the heavy lid up as far as it would go.

"Whew." I mopped my forehead again as we jumped to our feet. And peered into the open chest.

"No treasure," Shawn murmured, very disappointed.

"What *are* those?" I cried.

We were staring at little square boxes painted different colors. The whole trunk was stacked with these square boxes. Mostly blues and reds and purples.

I grabbed one off the top. It wasn't very heavy. I held it up to examine it. "Hey, check it out," I said, pushing it toward Shawn. "There's a crank on the side."

Shawn squinted at it. "It reminds me of that toy we had, remember? You turn the crank and it plays music, and then a clown pops up from the top?"

"It was a jack-in-the-box," I said. "When you were little, you loved it. You played with it for hours, making the clown pop up, then pushing him back in."

"Maybe this is a jack-in-the-box," Shawn said. "What are you waiting for, Violet? Turn the crank."

I wrapped my fingers around it. Then I hesitated. "Shawn, I . . . I suddenly have a weird feeling. Like we shouldn't turn the crank. Like there's something bad inside the box."

He groaned. "Violet, it looks just like the one we had. It's a toy. What's your problem?"

"My problem is that Uncle Jim locked it up and told us this is a forbidden room. So he probably knew something about these toys . . . something he wanted to keep away from everyone."

Shawn shook his head again. "How do you spell Violet?" he said. "W-I-M-P." He grabbed the box from my hands. He gripped it tightly with one hand, wrapped his fingers around the crank on the side, and began to turn it.

10

As Shawn turned the crank, music started to play. It sounded like someone plucking the strings of a tiny guitar, and it was playing the same song our old jack-in-the-box played— "Pop! Goes the Weasel."

"Shawn," I said, "do you think there's a law that *all* jack-in-the-boxes have to play 'Pop! Goes the Weasel'?"

I don't know if Shawn heard me. He was staring at the box in his hands, concentrating hard.

Then, suddenly, the music made a loud "POP!"

Shawn and I both cried out as the lid popped open and a chimp dressed in a white cap and white sailor's suit popped up on a spring. I laughed, watching the monkey puppet bob from side to side. "I knew it was going to pop open, but it surprised me anyway!"

Shawn grabbed the monkey's plastic head and

pushed it back into the box. He closed the lid. "I don't see what's so scary about this," he said. "It's just a baby toy."

I lifted another one out of the chest. This one looked older. The wood had a lot of cracks in it. The crank was bent.

I turned it slowly and it played the same song. As Shawn and I gazed at it, the words to the song played through my mind . . .

> *All around the mulberry bush,*
> *The monkey chased the weasel.*
> *The monkey thought 'twas all in good fun,*
> *POP! goes the weasel.*

The lid shot open, and the box nearly fell out of my hand. Up popped a sailor in a white sailor suit and cap. His little wooden right hand was pressed against his forehead in a salute.

"Cute," I said.

Shawn frowned. "I don't get it. So Uncle Jim collects jack-in-the-boxes. Why lock them up and tell us the room is forbidden?"

I laughed. "Maybe he's embarrassed that a big, tough sailor like him collects toys."

"Does that make any sense?" Shawn said. "I don't think so."

I shoved the sailor back into his box and snapped the lid shut.

Shawn and I tried a few more boxes. The next box held a woman pirate. She had long blond pigtails and red lipstick smeared all over her grinning face. She carried a tiny plastic skull in one hand.

More pirates popped out at us. One box had a *two-headed* pirate. One head was smiling. One head was frowning.

"That's a weird one," Shawn said. "Think it was a mistake?"

"No way," I replied. "Someone thought it was funny."

Almost all of the jack-in-the-boxes played "Pop! Goes the Weasel." A few of them played tunes we didn't recognize.

I tried cranking one box backward just to see what would happen. The song played backward, but a little pirate popped out anyway.

Shawn sighed. "This is getting boring. I don't see why we'll be in big trouble with Uncle Jim just because we played with a bunch of old jack-in-the-boxes."

We were nearly to the bottom of the chest. "Check this one out," I said. I leaned over the side of the trunk and pulled out an old-looking dark wood box. I raised it and blew a layer of dust off the top.

"This one doesn't have a crank," I said.

"Are you sure, Violet?" Shawn took it from my

hand and studied it carefully. "Here's a hole where the crank should go."

"Maybe it broke off," I said. Again, I leaned over the side of the chest and pawed around at the bottom. No sign of a crank.

"Maybe we could pull a crank off one of the other boxes and use it on this one," Shawn said.

I felt another heavy stab of dread in the pit of my stomach. A warning from somewhere.

"Shawn, maybe Uncle Jim doesn't want this one to open," I said. "Perhaps he took the crank off it. Maybe that's why he buried this box at the bottom under all the others."

Shawn ignored me. He had already pulled a metal crank off one of the other boxes. He jammed it into the side of this dusty, old box. "It looks like all the others," he said. "I don't know what you're afraid of."

I held my breath as he began to turn the crank.

"It's working," he said.

Music began to float out from inside the box. It wasn't "Pop! Goes the Weasel." It was deep and gloomy. Like horror-movie music.

"Shawn—stop," I said.

He kept cranking. The deep, scary music played. Shawn cranked faster. The music kept its low, steady drone.

"Hey, it should have popped open by now," Shawn said, frowning at it as he turned the crank.

"Maybe it's broken," I said. "Put it back in the chest. Okay, Shawn? Seriously—"

POP.

The lid popped up. And the room exploded in a deafening, shattering blast of thunder and smoke.

11

"Can't breathe . . ."

I coughed and choked in the swirls of thick black smoke. I shut my eyes, but I couldn't stop the burning tears from rolling down my face.

I held my breath as long as I could. I could hear Shawn choking beside me. But the smoke was so thick, I couldn't see him.

Finally, the black faded to gray, and the heavy blanket of smoke cleared. I wiped my wet eyes with both hands. I struggled to see through my tears.

Shawn had dropped to his knees on the floor. He hunched next to the box, which must have dropped from his hands. The lid stood open, and a pirate puppet bounced from side to side on its spring.

I dropped down beside my brother and put a hand on his shoulder. "Are you okay?"

He nodded. "That was a horrible explosion. Scared me to death."

"Me too," I said.

"Thanks for letting Jack the Knife out!" the little pirate shouted.

Shawn and I both gasped. "It talks!"

The pirate's mouth didn't move, but the voice was definitely coming from him. He tossed back his head and we heard a laugh, a hearty, loud laugh.

He wore a red bandanna over his black hair. A bright blue jacket over a black-and-white-striped shirt. He had large brown eyes and a long nose above a black mustache.

He carried a long-bladed knife in his right hand. His left hand was missing. A curled metal hook appeared in its place.

"Jack the Knife has been waiting many a year!" the little figure cried, bouncing on his spring. "Are you ready for a Jack Attack?"

A shudder ran down my spine. "Th-this is too creepy," I stammered. "Shawn, please—push him back in."

Shawn leaned over and spread his palm over the pirate's bandanna. He pushed down.

"Hey!"

He pushed harder. Then he raised his eyes to me. "It's stuck. It won't go back down."

The little pirate laughed again. "It's Jack Attack time! Jack the Knife is here to stay, mate!"

"Get back in!" I cried. I grabbed the box and pounded my fist on the pirate's head. I pounded and pushed. "Get back in! Get back."

"It's a Jack Attack! I won't go back!"

And as he said that, he began to grow.

"Whoa!"

Startled, I uttered a cry and jerked my hand away. I toppled onto my back as the pirate started to expand.

Bobbing on his spring, he raised himself out of the box. He stretched his arms at his sides as he rose.

Gaping in disbelief, I struggled to my feet. I gasped as I saw the metal spring disappear. The pirate figure grew legs. Black boots appeared at the bottoms of white sailor pants.

Shawn was still on his knees on the floor, staring up at the growing pirate, his eyes bulging in horror. I stumbled back.

The pirate swayed unsteadily on his black boots. He tilted forward, then back, gaining his balance. He loomed over Shawn and me, more than six feet tall.

His mustache flapped, his brown eyes flashed gleefully, and his mouth moved now.

"Are ye afraid of Jack the Knife?" he boomed. "You have good reason to be afraid!"

12

"This . . . This is *crazy!*" Shawn cried. He jumped to his feet and grabbed my arm. "Violet, what are we going to do?"

Jack the Knife tossed back his head and laughed, his brown eyes rolling around like marbles.

I brought my face close to Shawn's and whispered, "Come on. We're *outta* here."

I gazed around the room. The explosion had scattered the jack-in-the-boxes all over the floor.

I turned and started toward the door. But wait . . . it wasn't on the same wall. Somehow the room was all turned around. A heavy fisherman's net was draped over the door. That definitely hadn't been there before. How could this be?

I couldn't contain my fright. I opened my mouth and screamed. "Uncle Jim! Uncle Jim! Can you hear me?"

The pirate's grin didn't fade. "He can't hear you now, my girl."

I swung back to Jack. "Who *are* you?" I cried in a trembling voice. "What do you want?"

"You have to let us go," Shawn added almost in a whisper.

The pirate raised his arm and rubbed his mustache with the curled part of his hook. He lowered his gaze to the floor, and his eyes moved from box to box.

"Where are ye, mates?" he boomed. "Rise and shine, me hearties! Rise and shine, everyone! Are ye sailors or are ye lazy sons of a sea tortoise?"

I heard a rattling sound. And then *Pop! Pop! Pop!*

Boxes jumped and skittered across the floor as they popped open, one at a time. To my shock, the little puppets Shawn and I had seen sprang up.

They sprang up chattering, with tinny voices that rang off the walls and low ceiling. All talking at once. And as they talked, they began to grow.

Like Jack the Knife, they rose from their boxes, swinging from side to side on their springs. Their heads and bodies appeared to inflate, and their clothes stretched to fit them.

"Reporting for duty, Captain."

"Aye aye, sir."

"Top of the morning, mates."

"Time to ride the white-water waves."

Their voices deepened as they grew taller.

Shawn and I froze in horror as they stepped out of their little boxes, their boots clattering on the floor. The chimpanzee in a white sailor suit. The two-headed sailor. The blond woman with the long pigtails down her back. A pirate with a parrot on his shoulder.

"Welcome, mates!" Jack shouted, spreading his arms in greeting. "We sleep no more. The time for action has arrived."

The grown figures each tossed an arm into the air and cheered. The chimp made a hooting sound and bounced up and down on his hairy bare feet.

The two-headed sailor stepped forward. He was tall and thin and his sailor suit was baggy. It was much too big for him, but he had green suspenders to help hold his pants up. His heads were identical. They were completely bald, and had tiny black eyes over beak-like noses.

"Must be good weather for sailing," one head said.

"We don't need good weather to sail," the other head replied.

"Yes, we do."

"No, we don't."

"The weather is important to a sailing man."

"No, it isn't."

Jack the Knife stepped up and poked his hook

onto their chest. "Easy, me hearties. We're not the ones to be sailing today."

He turned to Shawn and me. "The one on the left is Salty Magee, a good sailing man if ever there was one. The one on the right goes by the name Pepper Magee. You won't find anyone better than Salty and Pepper."

The other sailors all shouted agreement.

The chimp hooted again. "Easy, Chuckles," Jack told him. "I've got a banana for you if you behave."

Chuckles grinned and bounced up and down.

Jack turned to the woman sailor. Her big, dark eyes darted back and forth nervously. "And how are ye today, Mad Madeline?" Jack demanded.

She tossed back her blond pigtails. "Go squeeze a frog and see if it burps," she replied.

Jack laughed. "Mad as ever, aren't ye, Madeline?"

She sneered at him. "Can you swallow a flounder without choking on it? I'd like to see you try."

Jack's smile faded. "Madeline, can you curtsy to your leader?"

She put her lips together and made a rude sound.

Some of the others laughed. But they stopped when Jack turned and scowled at them.

I realized my whole body was shaking. I took a deep breath and tried to sound calm. "Nice to meet you all," I said. "But my brother and I have to leave now."

"Well spoken, me girl," Jack replied. "But that isn't in the stars."

"In the stars?" I said. "What do you mean? Shawn and I have to go. Our Uncle Jim will be here any minute."

"Yes, he'll be looking for us," Shawn added, huddled close to me.

Some of the sailors laughed at that.

"Their uncle is looking for them," Salty Magee said.

"No, he isn't," Pepper Magee replied.

"We have other plans for you," Jack the Knife said, rubbing his cheek with the tip of his hook. "Dangerous plans, don't you know."

"Tusk tusk. My uncle was a walrus," Mad Madeline said. "Did you ever meet my Uncle Wally?"

"No, please," I pleaded. "Listen to me. We have to go back to our uncle—right now." Then Shawn and I cupped our hands around our mouths and started to scream: "Uncle Jim! Help us! Uncle Jim! Hurry!"

Some of the sailors laughed again. The chimp in the sailor suit scratched his head and grinned so wide, I could see his pink gums.

Jack shook his head, pretending to be sad. "A pity. The old admiral can't hear you," he said. "You see, he's not in a place where he can hear you."

I stared at him. "What do you mean? Where is our uncle?"

The pirate lifted a box off the floor and handed it to me. "Go ahead, Missy. Turn the crank."

"Don't do it," Shawn urged.

Jack the Knife stood over me. He had his hook raised in front of his chest. "Go ahead. Turn it. Let's hear the pretty music." He motioned to the other pirates. "Let's all sing along, mates."

"N-no," I stuttered. "I don't want to."

A low growl escaped Jack's lips. He lowered his hook to my shoulder and pressed it against me. "Turn it, Missy."

"Ow." I had no choice. I held the box in one trembling hand and began to turn the crank on the side. The music plunked, and the pirates all sang along with it:

> *All around the mulberry bush,*
> *The monkey chased the weasel.*
> *The monkey thought 'twas all in good fun,*
> *POP! goes the ADMIRAL.*

The lid flew open—and a large, white-haired figure in a white sailor suit and cap came shooting up. It bounced crazily around on its spring.

I gripped the box in both hands, brought it close to my face to study it—and screamed. "Uncle Jim!"

13

"Oh noooooo!" Shawn wailed beside me.

"What have you done to him? How did you do this?" I cried.

Jack tapped me on the shoulder again with his hook. "It's a fair trade, don't ye agree? An admiral for a captain?" He laughed.

Shawn and I stared in horror at the bouncing figure, the bulging stomach, the white hair falling from under his cap, the white mustache, our uncle's red face, frozen in an openmouthed scream of horror.

Jack the Knife stood watching us, a wide grin on his face. "As ye can see, your uncle can't come to your rescue."

"You—you can't *do* this!" I stammered.

"Captain Jack the Knife can do *anything*," Salty Magee said.

"No, he can't do everything," Pepper disagreed.

"Yes, he can."

"I beg to differ."

61

Jack raised his hook to stop the two-headed sailor from arguing with himself. He took the jack-in-the-box of Uncle Jim from my hands and handed it to another sailor.

"Would you like the old admiral back?" he asked Shawn and me. "Would you like everything to go back to normal?"

I didn't answer the question. I signaled Shawn with my eyes. "Run!" I whispered.

We both took off, running toward the far wall. If we could shove aside the heavy net that covered the door, perhaps we could escape.

Jack and his pirates, startled by our sudden move, froze for a moment. I hurtled past him, dodged Mad Madeline, and dove toward the net.

"Head for the lighthouse, Shawn," I called. "Maybe we'll be safe there."

"No, you won't," said Salty Magee, springing to life.

"Yes, they will," said Pepper, his other head. "Stop them!"

"*You* stop them!" Salty shouted.

"*You* stop them!" Pepper shot back.

The two-headed sailor spread his arms, preparing to tackle us.

Shawn ducked to the right. I ducked to the left. And we darted right past him. He spun around. Too late.

The shouts of Jack and his pirates rang out behind us. Shawn and I were nearly to the net on the wall. I could see the door behind it clearly now.

I dove for the door—when I heard Shawn's cry.

I turned and saw the big chimp tackle Shawn from behind. With a loud grunt, Shawn went down on his belly. Chuckles hopped onto Shawn's back and began jumping up and down on him.

"Noooo!" A cry escaped my throat.

"Clambake on the beach! Clambake on the beach!" Mad Madeline was screaming. *Did she ever make any sense at all?*

I lowered my shoulder and bumped the chimp hard. Chuckles toppled off Shawn and struggled to catch his balance. That gave me just enough time to grab Shawn's hand and pull him to his feet.

"Clambake on the beach!" I heard Mad Madeline's cry behind us as we reached the net. Shawn and I both frantically tore at the net, struggling to push it aside.

"Stop them! Stop them, you lugs!" Jack was screaming.

The pirates closed in. Hands grabbed for us. I ducked my shoulder, tried to squirm free.

The net fell away, and I grabbed the doorknob, twisted it—and Shawn and I burst through.

We ducked our heads and kept running. The angry shouts and cries followed close behind us.

Whoa! Wait a minute!

The door didn't lead back to the room with all

of Uncle Jim's treasures. We were *outside*! Shawn and I were running through tall grass.

Breathing hard, my heart pounded so fast, my chest ached. I saw the blue-green ocean ahead of us, sparkling under the low afternoon sun.

"Where is the lighthouse?" Shawn cried.

We both spun in a circle. No sign of the lighthouse. It was gone! But that was *impossible*.

The house, I realized, was different. This house was built of dark stone and had black shutters over all the windows.

"Everything has changed!" I cried. I couldn't keep my voice from trembling. I gasped breath after breath. "We did this, Shawn. When we opened the jack-in-the-box. Don't you see? We changed *everything*!"

We heard shouts from the house and then clomping footsteps.

We turned and started to run again. A narrow dirt path led down to the beach. And to our left, I saw the wood plank dock, the dock that Uncle Jim's tiny boat had been moored at.

"Oh no!" A cry escaped my throat as I saw the big sailing ship anchored at the dock now. Not our uncle's tiny speedboat. But a two-masted sailing ship *with black sails*.

A pirate ship!

The pirates came after us, blocking our getaway. We had no choice. Shawn and I ran onto the dock. Our shoes thudded loudly on the wood planks. The little dock swayed under our footsteps.

Waves splashed up against both sides of the narrow dock. I felt the cold spray on my skin. Wave after wave crashed over the shore. High clouds dotted the afternoon sky.

Panting for breath, we ran to the end of the dock. Surrounded by rolling waves now. Nothing but the ocean and the enormous pirate ship, bobbing in the water to our right.

Trapped.

Nowhere to run.

The pirates closed in on us, led by Jack the Knife. They didn't even have to run. They knew they had us trapped on the dock.

Shawn and I exchanged frantic glances. Should we jump into the ocean?

No. We weren't strong swimmers. Besides, there was nowhere we could swim to safety.

My heart pounded as we stood side by side on the edge of the dock. Water splashing up on three sides of us. The dock trembling under the weight of all of us as we watched Jack and his pirates move closer, already grinning in triumph.

"Are they going to push us into the water?" Shawn asked in a tiny voice. I could barely hear him over the pounding waves.

A wave crashed over my feet, sending a shiver of cold up my body. I kept my eyes on Jack as he led his pirates toward us. He had a jagged knife raised in his hand, the blade gleaming in the red afternoon sunlight. His hook was raised menacingly. He was ready for battle.

"Please—" I stuttered as he stepped up close. "Please—"

Shawn pressed against me. Nowhere to back away. Our heels were already over the edge of the dock. One push and we'd be in the tossing waters.

Jack lowered his knife. His eyes were on me. "I believe I asked a question before you decided to leave so rudely, my girl."

I swallowed. "A . . . a question?"

He nodded. "I believe I asked if ye would like to get your uncle back? If ye would like to return to your old life?"

"Yes. Yes. Definitely yes," I answered breathlessly.

"Yes. How can we get Uncle Jim back? Tell us," Shawn cried.

Jack rubbed his chin with his hook. "Well . . . listen carefully," he said. "There's only one way you can do it."

14

The pirates circled us and forced us back into the house. The jack-in-the-boxes, their lids standing open, were still scattered over the floor.

Jack's pirates sat on the floor with their backs against one wall. Mad Madeline paced in front of them, her pigtails flying behind her.

"Sit ye down, Maddy," Jack ordered.

"Go sit on a one-legged parrot," she replied. She tossed back her head and laughed as if she had made a great joke.

Salty and Pepper took her arm gently and helped her sit down.

Shawn and I stood in the middle of the room, our arms crossed in front of us. I felt a little safer away from the edge of the dock. But a chill lingered at the back of my neck as I waited to hear Jack's words.

He adjusted the red bandanna over his long, straight black hair. His dark eyes moved from Shawn to me. His expression was serious.

"If ye want to save old Admiral Jim and return to your life as ye knew it . . ." He gestured with his hook as he talked. "It be simple."

"Simple Simon ate a pie man!" Mad Madeline shouted from her place against the wall.

Chuckles the chimp hooted, as if he thought that was funny.

"Wh-what do we have to do?" I stammered.

"Sail to Clam Island," Jack answered. He waited for Shawn and me to react. But we just stood there, staring blankly back at him.

"It's a short journey if you follow the sun," Jack said.

"No, it isn't," Pepper Magee chimed in.

"Yes, it is," his other head argued.

"We have to sail to an island?" I said, trying to make sense of his words.

Jack nodded. "Sail to Clam Island and rescue Captain Pip."

Shawn and I exchanged glances. "Who is Captain Pip?" I asked.

"My canary," Jack said. "Pip was kidnapped by canary kidnappers, and I want him back."

"So Shawn and I go to Clam Island and bring back your canary?"

"No," Mad Madeline interrupted. "You sail to Canary Island and bring back his clam." She tossed back her head and laughed again.

"It be that simple," Jack said, ignoring her. "If

68

you bring back Captain Pip, I promise—on a pirate's honor—to go back in my box. And all my crew will disappear, too. And Admiral Jim will return. All will be normal again."

"But—but—" Shawn sputtered.

I pictured the huge ship at the dock with its tall masts and wide black sails. "It's impossible. Shawn and I aren't sailors," I said. "We can't sail a ship by ourselves."

Jack rolled his dark eyes. "Of course you can't. Think Jack the Knife be a fool? That's why I be sending a crew with you."

I glanced at the pirates sitting against the wall. "A crew?"

Jack nodded. He pointed with his hook. "Salty and Pepper will be going with ye. And Chuckles. And Madeline. The best crew a sailor could ask for."

Was he joking?

No. As he pointed to them, the three pirates jumped to their feet and saluted. "Aye aye," Salty said.

"Nay nay," Pepper replied.

"You're supposed to say *aye aye*," Salty corrected him.

"You're not the boss of me," Pepper shot back.

Chuckles the chimp tugged at his sailor cap, rolled his tongue over his teeth, and jumped up and down excitedly.

69

Madeline cleared her throat for attention. "I'd like to sing my favorite farewell song now. But I'm sad because I don't know the words." She wiped a tear from one eye.

Shawn leaned closer to me and whispered, "We can't sail with them. No way. They're all crazy."

I turned to Jack. "Do we have a choice? Is there anything else Shawn and I could do to convince you to go back in your jack-in-the-boxes?"

"Captain Pip is a lov-er-ly canary," he replied. "When the little birdie sings, it sends a warm fluttering to my heart."

"Yes," I said, "but . . . why can't you get him yourself?"

"Because I'm allergic," Jack replied. "Allergic to clams. I get such a rash, you wouldn't believe."

"But you could stay on the ship and your crew—" I started. But Jack raised his hook to silence me.

"You want to see your uncle again, don't ye?" he snapped angrily. "Ye want all of us to go back in our boxes, don't ye? Then set sail for Clam Island today on the *Jolly Sea Scab*, and bring back my Pip—and stop jabbering."

I swallowed. I stood up taller to keep my legs from trembling.

"The *Jolly Sea Scab*?" Shawn said in a tiny voice. "Is that really the name of your ship?"

A grin slowly spread over Jack's face. "It's

the Scab of the Sea," he boasted, "known far and wide."

A few minutes later, Shawn and I were walking up the gangplank, boarding the big ship as it bobbed against the dock. The wooden deck stood high above the water. The black sails flapped noisily above our heads in a strong, steady breeze.

Salty and Pepper, Chuckles, and Madeline followed us on board. Chuckles was hooting and grunting and hopping up and down, very excited.

Shawn gazed around the deck. I grabbed the rail and turned back to the shore. I could see Jack the Knife peering up at us from the rocky beach behind the dock. And I could see the house beyond the reeds.

"Hoist anchor!" Salty Magee shouted.

"*You* do it!" Pepper snapped back.

"No. *You* do it!"

I heard a grinding sound. Soon after, I saw the big metal anchor rise up from the water. The ship bobbed free of the dock. We were setting sail. No turning back now.

Waves splashed against the sides of the ship as we began to move.

Peering down at the shore, I saw a dark spot at the foot of the dock. It took a few seconds to realize it was Celeste. Yes. The black cat was staring up at us as we began to move.

And over the wind, I could hear the cat's cry: *"Don't go! Don't go!"*

SLAPPY HERE, EVERYONE . . .

If you ask me, Celeste is a *scaredy-cat*.

What's so frightening about sailing off in a pirate ship to a faraway island with a two-headed sailor, a chimp, and a crazy pirate? The only thing missing is a talking dummy.

I'd like to go on a sailing ship. I'd love to see giant tuna fish swimming in the sea. One thing I always wondered about tuna fish: How do they squeeze themselves into those tiny little cans? Haha.

Well, Violet and her brother are going to meet tougher creatures than tuna fish. I hope Violet's new nickname isn't *Shark Bait*!

Hahaha.

15

Shawn and I stood side by side, our hands gripping the railing above the deck. The ship bounced on the low waves. The sails fluttered and snapped as they caught the wind, and we picked up speed.

We didn't speak as we watched the dock and the beach and the house grow smaller and smaller, fading into the distance.

There was no reason to speak. No one to call for help. No one to rescue us from this crazy mission.

Sail to an island? Capture a canary and bring it back?

Of course, the whole thing was impossible.

The black sails whistled and snapped, as if greeting the wind. The air smelled salty and felt cold against my burning cheeks.

"Wonder if we'll ever see Uncle Jim again," I said to Shawn.

He sighed. "Wonder if we'll ever see *Mom and Dad* again," he murmured.

"It's all our fault," I said. "If only we had listened to Uncle Jim. If only we had stayed out of that locked room."

Shawn swallowed hard and made a gulping sound. He shook his head sadly and didn't reply.

The waves rose higher. Water splashed onto the deck, rolling over our shoes. We both leaped back. The wind blew our hair wildly about our heads.

"How long do you think it will take to get to the island?" Shawn asked in a tiny, frightened voice.

I had no idea, so I just shrugged my shoulders.

"I'm going down below," he said, pointing to a narrow stairway leading down. "See if I can find our cabin."

I started to follow him, but Salty and Pepper stepped into my path. The two heads studied the waves beyond the deck.

The ship rocked hard and the deck tilted up. I lost my balance and stumbled into him. He staggered to the side, and we both nearly fell over.

"Easy," Salty said. He took me by my shoulders and stood me upright. "It will take a while to get your sea legs."

"No, it won't," Pepper said.

"Yes, it will. Why do you always argue with me?"

"I don't," Pepper replied.

"Yes, you do."

Both heads turned to me. "Which way to Clam Island?" Salty asked.

I gasped. "Which way? Why are you asking *me*?"

"Because I don't know," he replied.

"I don't know, either," Pepper said.

Those words sent a stab of fear into my heart. Were we lost already?

"Follow the moon," a voice said from the stairway. Mad Madeline appeared from the deck below.

The two heads spun to her. "Follow the moon? It's the middle of the afternoon."

"Follow the moon," she repeated. "It will never lead you wrong." She took her braids and tied them in a double knot.

A wave of panic swept over me. I forced myself to speak. "You really don't know the way to Clam Island?" I said in a trembling voice.

"I believe it's that way," Salty said. His left hand pointed right. His right hand pointed left.

"Omigosh," I uttered. "Well . . . who is steering the ship?"

"Look on the captain's bridge," he replied. He pointed to a raised deck at the back of the ship.

I saw Chuckles the chimp standing up there. He had a banana in one hand and the big wooden ship's wheel in the other. He was spinning the wheel one way, then the other.

"The chimp is steering the ship?" I cried, unable to hold down my total panic.

"He doesn't know where we're going," Madeline chimed in. "But we're making good speed."

"Why?" I demanded. "Why is Chuckles steering the ship?"

Salty spoke in a low voice. "Do you want to be the one to tell him he *can't*?"

"But you're a sailor, right?" I cried. "You've sailed on this ship many times? And you really don't know how to guide us to the island?"

He shrugged. Both heads shook *no*. "I've been sailing all my life . . ." Salty started.

"No, you haven't," Pepper interrupted.

"I've been sailing all my life, but directions have always been a mystery to me."

"Me too," Pepper added.

I blinked. *Did they just agree on something?*

The ship rocked again. Bursts of wind sent my hair flying straight back. I shivered.

I was trapped on a ship with these lunatics. Already lost on the ocean. The ship was being guided by a chimpanzee in a sailor suit. And no one had a clue how to navigate us to where we were going.

Where was Shawn? I had to tell him we were in worse trouble than we had imagined.

Just as these thoughts swept through my panicked mind, my brother appeared in the stairway from below. He pushed past Madeline and stumbled toward me across the deck.

"Look what I found in the cabin below," Shawn cried. He raised a rolled-up sheet of canvas in one hand. "It's a map."

"Really?" I cried. "A map that shows the way to Clam Island?"

Shawn nodded. "Yes. It has all these lines drawn on it. And one line goes straight to Clam Island."

"Oh, thank goodness!" I said. "Thank goodness! A map!"

Shawn held it up and started to unroll it.

"Let me see that," Salty said. He grabbed it out of Shawn's hands.

"No. Let *me* see it!" Pepper shouted.

The map went from one hand to the other.

"I saw it first!" Salty exclaimed.

"Let me see it!" Pepper cried.

The left hand grabbed it. Then the right hand grabbed it back.

The two hands appeared to fight over it.

"Give it to me!"

"Let me see it!"

A strong blast of wind sent the rolled-up map flying out of their hands.

"Oh noooooo!" I screamed as I watched the map sail over the railing, plunge down into the water, and disappear in the waves.

16

I grabbed the rail and gazed down into the water. My stomach felt as if ocean waves were tossing inside me. I had to force myself to breathe.

I turned back to the others. "*Now* what are we going to do?" I cried. "What will we do without a map?"

"Follow the moon," Madeline said. "It's all so easy if you follow the moon."

Up on the captain's bridge, I saw Chuckles start another banana. He had one hand on the wheel, spinning it one way, then the other.

"It's all your fault," Pepper told his other head.

"No. Your fault," Salty replied.

"Without a map, we're lost," I moaned, shaking my head sadly.

"No, we're not," Shawn said. "I think we are okay."

Everyone turned to him. "Shawn, what do you mean?" I asked.

"I memorized the map," he answered. "At least, I think I did."

"I memorized the map, too," Madeline said. "But I never saw it. I memorized it without seeing it."

"Clam Island is directly northeast of here," Shawn said. "If we follow a straight line northeast, we will find it."

"Sorry," Salty said, "but sailors don't say *northeast*. You have to say nor' east. If you don't say nor' east, we don't know what you're talking about."

"Not true," Pepper argued.

"We need someone to steer us nor' east," I said. "I don't think Chuckles can do it."

I glanced at the captain's bridge. Chuckles was standing on his head now, scratching his stomach.

"Of *course* Chuckles can't do it," Salty said. "Chuckles is a chimpanzee."

"Well, I can man the wheel," Pepper said. "I steered many a sailing ship to shore."

"No, you haven't," Salty told his other head.

"I can try," Pepper replied.

Madeline climbed up to the bridge. She took Chuckles by the hand and led him down. "Chuckles and I are going down to my cabin to have a chat."

"Hoot hoot hoot," said Chuckles.

"Maybe we'll play a game of chess," Madeline said.

"Hoot hoot."

"I know what you're saying," she told Chuckles. "You don't enjoy it because I always win. But that's because you're a chimp and you don't know the rules."

I watched them disappear down the stairs.

Salty and Pepper climbed up to the bridge and took the wheel. They moved it steadily between their hands.

As Shawn and I watched, the two heads tilted up toward the sky and began to sing a sea song into the wind, loud and strong.

We're salty dogs, salty dogs are we,
And like salty dogs everywhere, we sail
*   the salty sea.*
We sail the salty sea
We sail the salty sea,
We're salty dogs, yes, salty dogs,
And where the rolling waves take us,
Salty dogs we be.

Salty sang the melody, and Pepper sang harmony, and it sounded pretty good.

The sun was red now, lowering itself so low, it appeared to be sinking into the tossing waters. High clouds swept slowly above us. The water shimmered and sparkled as we moved over it.

I started to feel a little better. If Shawn read the map correctly, we were on the right course. And Salty Magee seemed to know how to handle the wheel.

I turned to Shawn, who was staring out at the blazing colors of the setting sun. "Maybe we'll get lucky," I said. "Maybe we can get to that island and back."

"Maybe," Shawn said.

Our luck held for another ten minutes. Then the ship sprung a leak.

17

Shawn and I stood at the railing, gazing down at the tossing green waters. Up on the bridge, Salty and Pepper sang their song for at least the tenth time as they guided the wheel.

The air had grown cooler, and strong gusts ruffled my hair. I was thinking of going down to our cabin below when I heard sounds in the stairway.

Chuckles appeared first, followed by Madeline. I gasped when I saw they were both dripping wet. "What happened?" I cried.

Madeline squeezed water from her hair. She grinned at me. "Chuckles and I, we were swimming."

Shawn's eyes were bulging out of his head. "Swimming?"

Madeline nodded. "Yes. Swimming in the pool down below."

Above us, Salty and Pepper let go of the ship's wheel and started to climb down from the bridge.

"Swimming pool?" Salty barked. "We don't *have* a swimming pool on this ship."

Madeline's mouth dropped open. "Oh, I see. Then there must be a leak."

Chuckles hooted and scratched the wet fur on his chest.

Salty leaped to the deck. Both heads let out cries of alarm.

Shawn and I started toward the stairway. But the ship suddenly tilted up on a strong wave. We lost our balance and stumbled back to the railing.

Salty and Pepper were already in the stairwell. I heard their shoes clumping down the wooden steps. And then I heard their horrified scream from down below. "Sinking! The *Jolly Sea Scab* is sinking!"

I grabbed Shawn's hand. The wind blew my hair into my face. I forced myself to breathe. Panic choked my throat.

Madeline shook her head. "I should have remembered. No pool on board." She slapped her forehead. "What was I thinking?"

Shawn's eyes were still wide. His face had gone pale. He squeezed my hand. "Violet? Are we all going to drown?"

Before I could answer, Salty and Pepper jumped back up on deck. The legs of their sailor pants were soaked through. "We're not going to drown," Salty answered Shawn.

"Yes, we are," Pepper said, his voice trembling.

"No, we're not," Salty insisted. "We have a lifeboat—remember?"

"Yes, you're right," Pepper said. "I forgot."

"You didn't forget, Pepper. You just like to argue."

"No, I don't."

"STOP ARGUING, you two!" I screamed. "Where is the lifeboat? Get us to the lifeboat!"

"I think it's tea time," Madeline said. She checked her pocket watch, even though she didn't have a pocket or a watch. "Can we have a nice cup of tea before we hit the lifeboat?"

The ship tilted again, and we were all thrown together in a heap.

"We . . . we're definitely sinking," Shawn murmured. "I . . . I don't like this, Violet."

"No time for tea," Salty told Madeline. "We are going down fast. We have to man the lifeboat. Follow me!"

"Follow *me*!" Pepper said.

Holding on to the deck rail as the ship sank in the waves, Shawn and I followed to the other end of the ship. I saw the lifeboat hanging above the deck on thick ropes.

It was a long, narrow rowboat with oars hooked onto both sides. Salty shoved the boat over the side of the ship's deck. Then he began untying knots in the ropes. "I'll have the boat in the water in no time," he said.

Chuckles screeched. He slapped Shawn on the back enthusiastically.

It didn't take more than a few minutes. Salty freed the ropes and the rowboat dropped with a loud splash into the rolling ocean below.

Shawn and I peered down at it. It looked so tiny, bobbing in the deep green waves along the side of our sinking ship.

"How do we get down to it?" I asked.

Salty heaved a rope ladder over the side. "Ye climb down and ye'll be safe as clam chowder."

I swallowed. My heart was beating hard. That rowboat looked a long way down. The ship was rocking and tilting as it sank. Would I be able to hold on to the rope ladder and lower myself safely?

Chuckles hopped up and down excitedly. Madeline shook her head. "I left my favorite nose whistle down below. Can I go get it?"

"No time," Salty said, pushing her toward the rope ladder. "Ye know the rule of the sea. Women and children first."

"Yes. Women and children first," Pepper said, definitely agreeing with his other head this time.

Madeline stepped aside. She grabbed me by the shoulders and moved me to the top of the rope ladder. "Women and children first," she repeated. "Down you go, Violet. Happy landings."

Now my heart was beating so hard, my chest ached. My muscles all froze. I grabbed the side ropes of the ladder. My hands were shaking so hard, I could barely grip them.

I turned and lowered my shoes to the first rung of the ladder. Shawn leaned over the side. "Good luck, Violet. You can do it. I'll be right behind you."

The ship tossed and I nearly lost my hold on the ladder. I gasped and gripped the rough rope tighter. I started to lower one foot to the next rung.

"You can do it. You can do it!" Shawn called after me.

But I stopped when I saw Chuckles leap onto the ship's railing above me. The big chimp balanced on the railing. Bent his knees. Once. Twice.

Then he leaped off the railing, over the side of the ship.

Gripping the rope ladder, I watched him fall. His arms high over his head, he plunged straight down. He landed inside the lifeboat with a loud crash and thud. The rowboat bounced high in the water, then splashed back down.

Above me, Salty and Pepper, Madeline, and Shawn were all shouting at once. Clinging to the ladder, I watched the chimp sit up in the small boat.

Chuckles pulled himself toward the back of the boat. He grabbed the oars on both sides of him.

And as we all shouted for him to stop, he leaned forward and began to row.

Then, suddenly, we all were quiet. All gazing down at the deep green waters. All watching in horror as Chuckles rowed merrily away in the only lifeboat.

18

Shawn grabbed my hands and helped pull me off the ladder, back onto the ship. My legs were shaking so hard, I could barely stand. I grabbed the railing to hold myself up.

The bow of the ship tilted up as the stern sank lower. We huddled at the back, getting closer and closer to the water.

"We ... we're stuck on this sinking ship," Shawn whispered.

I put a hand on his shoulder. His whole body was shaking. His teeth were chattering. Ocean spray splashed over us. The sound of the waves grew louder as we sank lower and lower, closer and closer to the churning sea. Our black sails whipped angrily in the blowing wind.

Salty Magee raised a hand to get our attention. "Don't panic, everybody. No reason to panic."

"Why shouldn't we panic?" Pepper asked. "I think we should definitely panic."

The ship jerked hard. Icy water splashed over us.

"Maybe you're right," Salty said. "Okay. Go ahead and panic, everyone."

"What about the raft?" Madeline chimed in. "Don't we have a life raft on board?"

"Of course we do," Salty replied. "I should have remembered. We have a raft down below. Our lives have been saved!"

He dove for the stairway and disappeared below. Shawn and I gripped the rail with both hands. Our shoes were slipping and sliding on the deck as the ship tilted higher. I knew that in a short while, we would slide into the sea.

"Wh-what's taking him so long?" Shawn demanded.

Salty climbed back on deck, shaking his head. "No raft," he said. "The hold is filled with water. But there's no raft down there. Nothing."

I let out a long sigh.

"Well . . . we could make a raft," Madeline said, stepping up to him. "If we have a saw, we can cut a raft big enough for the four of us. We can cut it out of the deck."

"Good idea," he said.

"I don't think so," Pepper said.

"Find a saw in the supply cabin," Madeline told Salty. "We don't have much time."

Salty turned and ran across the tilted deck. I stepped up to Madeline. "That was a great idea," I said. "You—you're making sense," I blurted out.

She brought her face close to mine and whispered: "I'm not really crazy, Violet. It's all an act. I act like this so Jack the Knife and the others won't put me to work. I don't want to be a pirate like them. Safer, you know."

I realized my mouth was hanging open. Shawn was staring at her, too.

All an act. Well ... she was a good actress. She had everyone fooled.

We cried out as the ship lurched again. I heard a cracking sound—and saw the rail on the deck wall crack and splinter. Glass shattered. The black sails flapped louder on their tilted masts.

Salty came running back to us. "We don't have a saw," he reported. "So we can't build a raft." He squinted at Madeline. "Any other ideas?"

Before she could answer, there was a deafening *craaaash*. One of the masts toppled over. The sails plunged into the waves, and the whole mast broke off and disappeared into the sea.

Cracking sounds ... shattering glass ... wood breaking ... crunching ... The deck shot away, tilted up, and we were standing on air.

I grabbed onto Shawn as we went flying, flying, then dropping, dropping ... hurling straight down ... into the water, both of us screaming all the way.

19

The slap of the water cut off my scream. My body plunged under the surface, and I sank with my eyes wide open. The icy chill of the water paralyzed me. I felt as if I'd sink forever.

I finally remembered that I had arms and legs. Fighting the cold and my panic, I shot my arms out and began to kick. My shoes were heavy under the water, and I kicked slowly, painfully, twisting my head up and reaching with both hands for the surface.

My head bobbed over the rolling waves, and I gasped for breath, my chest about to burst. The cold of the water sent chill after chill down my body. My clothes weighed me down. I felt as if I weighed four hundred pounds!

The salt water burned my eyes. I swallowed a mouthful and started to choke. Paddling furiously, I kept my head above the surface. "Shawn? Shawn?" I tried to shout his name, but my voice came out weak and muffled by the rush of tossing waters.

Frantically, I spun around. "Shawn?"

I didn't see him. I saw pieces of the boat floating on top of the water. Chunks of the masts. A black sail. Boxes and chests and chairs from the cabins down below.

"Shawn?" My voice cracked with terror. "Where *are* you?"

A wave tossed me backward. I hit something hard.

"Hey—!" a voice cried out.

I spun and saw my brother, his blond hair matted against his head, his eyes wide with terror, paddling hard, struggling to tread water as the waves pushed us one way, then the other.

"Shawn—you're okay!" I choked out.

"Violet—" I couldn't hear what he said. I knew that Shawn wasn't a very strong swimmer. I wrapped my hands around his waist and tried to hold him above the surface.

"We—we can't hold on much longer," Shawn said. A wave tossed us into the black sail floating on the surface. The sail sank slowly, silently. I held on to Shawn, and we bobbed away from it.

I pointed. "Look. The ship is gone. It's under the waves. Where are the others? Where are Madeline and Salty and Pepper?"

Shawn didn't seem to hear me. His whole body

shuddered under the water. "We . . . we're going to drown," he murmured.

"No," I said. "Hold on, Shawn. Keep kicking. Hold on."

I tried to sound courageous. But I knew Shawn was right. There was no way we could survive for long.

I held on to Shawn as a strong wave swept us forward. The sun was nearly down. I saw ripples of red light in the darkening water. The sky above us was gray with heavy, low clouds.

I spun in the water—and screamed when I saw Madeline and Salty and Pepper. They appeared to be floating on the surface of the water. Sitting up and floating toward us.

I blinked and blinked again. I knew I was seeing things. My terror was causing me to imagine them floating on the ocean crests.

But no.

They began to wave their arms and shout at us. And I saw they weren't floating by themselves. They were sitting on a square piece of the deck. They had a raft after all!

Salty and Pepper reached both hands down and grabbed Shawn under the shoulders. "Would ye like a ride?" he shouted. "Plenty of room for all."

Shawn scrambled onto the small raft. Then they pulled me on after him.

For a long moment, we all sat staring at one another. Shawn and I were breathing hard, water rolling down our faces. I shivered and hugged myself. The air had grown cold with the sun nearly down, and my soaked clothes pressed against my skin.

"The *Jolly Sea Scab* is at the bottom of the sea," Salty said. "She was a good ship."

"No, she wasn't," his other head replied. "She sprung a leak and stranded us here."

"She was a good ship in her day," Salty said.

Pepper muttered something I couldn't hear over the rush of wind and the steady wash of the waves.

"The deck made a good raft after all," Madeline said. She leaned back, pressing her hands on the wood planks behind her. "We didn't have to saw it. It broke into the perfect size."

"It doesn't matter," Salty said, shaking his head. "Look around. Nothing but ocean for miles. No other ship. No one to save us."

"We can't give up," I said. "Maybe—"

"We're going to freeze to death," Salty said. He shuddered.

"No, we're not," Pepper chimed in. "We're going to *starve* to death."

"Freeze to death," Salty insisted.

"Starve to death," Pepper said.

"Freeze to death!"

"That argument is not going to help us,"

94

Madeline said. "I don't care which one of you wins. You're not being helpful."

The two heads stared at her. "What *would* be helpful?" Pepper asked.

"*This* will," Madeline replied. She reached into a deep pocket in her skirt and pulled out a silvery pistol. She raised the gun in front of her.

"What are you going to do with that?" Salty cried. He raised his hands above his head as if in surrender.

"I—I *knew* you were crazy, Mad Madeline," Pepper sputtered. "But I didn't think you were *that* crazy."

"Put it down! Put it down!" Salty cried. "What do you think you are doing?"

I was holding my breath, my eyes on the pistol. Shawn had backed up to the edge of the raft.

A wave lifted us, carried us for a bit, then lowered us down hard.

Madeline grinned at Shawn and me. Then she turned to Salty, who still had his hands raised in the air. "It's a flare pistol," she said. "It's not a gun."

Both Salty and Pepper let out sighs of relief. They lowered their hands to the wooden raft.

"I grabbed this when the ship was going down," Madeline said. "I'm going to send up a flare. It will burst open, bright red against the gray sky. If there's a ship around anywhere, they'll see it. And they'll come rescue us from this flimsy raft."

Salty and Pepper both cheered. "Yes. Do it! Do it!" They both cried.

"Someone will see it," I said, trying to sound brave. "I *know* they will."

"Okay. Here goes." Madeline raised the flare gun above her head. She pointed it straight up at the sky.

The trigger made a loud click as she pulled it.

I raised my eyes to see the flare spread light over the sky.

But nothing happened.

Madeline kept the flare gun raised high. She pulled the trigger again.

Nothing.

She let out a groan and lowered the gun to her lap. "Guess it got wet," she murmured, shaking her head. "It doesn't work if it's wet."

The four of us sat staring at the flare gun in her lap.

Finally, Salty broke the silence. "That was our last chance," he said.

20

The sun dropped quickly. The sky grew as black as the waters that surrounded us.

The four of us sat hunched close together, hugging ourselves for warmth. There was no room to stretch out or lie down. Salty tried pushing his legs straight out, and his boots trailed in the water.

Madeline's head was down, and her hair covered her face. I couldn't tell if she was sleeping or not.

Shawn leaned his head against my shoulder and shut his eyes. My teeth were chattering. I tried to think warm thoughts. I thought about a sandy beach in sunlight. And about big steaming bowls of chicken soup.

It actually helped a little.

The raft slid up and down on the waves. The ocean was pretty gentle, but I still felt as if I was riding an endless roller coaster. My stomach growled. I lowered my head and shut my eyes, but I knew I couldn't sleep.

This is the worst night of my life, I told myself. *It can't get any worse than this.*

That's when I felt a hard bump. Something jolted the raft, lifting it off the water.

"Huh?"

"What's that?"

All four of us were alert now, gazing around frantically.

Another hard bump sent the raft sliding off a wave. I gripped the planks, pressing my hands into the wood. My entire body stiffened in fright.

"Sh-sharks," Shawn stuttered.

Another bump made me scream.

Madeline placed a hand on my shoulder. "Let them have their fun. They'll swim away soon. Sharks never stay still."

"But what if they're *hungry*?" I demanded.

"Don't put your hands or feet in the water to find out," Salty chimed in.

Another bump from under the raft made us all scream.

I bounced hard. Shawn grabbed me and held on to my arm.

"Does anyone know the Pirate's Prayer?" Pepper asked. "I'd like to say the Pirate's Prayer now."

"There's no such thing," Salty said.

"Too bad," Pepper said. "This would be a good time for it."

I was gritting my teeth so hard, my jaw ached. I hugged myself tightly, as if that could keep me safe. I squinted into the black water, trying to see the shark that kept attacking us.

But it was too dark to see anything. Too dark to see where the water ended and the sky began.

I'm not going to cry, I told myself. For one thing, it was too cold to cry. I imagined my tears freezing, turning to ice on my cheeks.

I have to be brave for Shawn.

He clung to my arm, his head down, his shoulders trembling.

"The shark is gone," I whispered. "Shawn—do you see? It's not bumping the raft anymore."

He didn't raise his head. "That's good," he whispered. "But Salty and Pepper are right. We can't survive out here."

I wanted to reply with something cheerful or optimistic. But I couldn't think of anything. So I just patted his arm and stayed silent.

How did we survive that dreadful night?

I don't know. I must have fallen asleep somehow. When I opened my eyes, a red ball of a sun was climbing the purple-pink sky. Beams of light trickled through the ocean waters.

I blinked myself alert. My arms and legs felt stiff. My hair had matted over my face.

I brushed it away—and saw a sailing ship in the distance.

"Hey—!" I gave a hoarse shout. My throat was still clogged from sleep. "Hey—look!"

Madeline raised her head and turned toward where I was pointing. Salty and Pepper had been snoring loudly together. They coughed themselves awake and stared at the ship.

"It has black sails!" Shawn exclaimed.

"Another pirate ship!" Salty cried. "Come to rescue us."

"Does it see us?" Pepper demanded.

The two-headed sailor jumped to his feet. He began shouting at the ship and jumping up and down.

"Easy! Easy!" Madeline warned. "You'll tip us over!" But she jumped up and began waving both arms frantically at the approaching ship.

The black sails seemed to grow larger as the big ship broke through the waves, sweeping toward us.

"We're going to be saved!" I cried. "I don't believe it. It's coming to rescue us!"

Shawn and I cheered as the hull of the ship bounced in the water. White waves rolled off the pirate ship's sides as it picked up speed.

Salty and Madeline were still on their feet, waving wildly to the ship.

"They see us!" Salty cried. "Yes! They see us!"

"No, they don't!" Pepper shouted. "They don't see us! Look out!"

Pepper was right.

I gasped in horror and grabbed on to Shawn. "They don't see us! They're going to crash right into us!"

SLAPPY HERE, EVERYONE . . .

I *hate* when that happens. When a ship crashes into you and you drown instantly. Don't you hate that, too?

Thank goodness the story doesn't end here. I don't think that ending would make a splash with anyone. Haha.

What do you think happens now? I don't know. I get a SINKING feeling when I think about it. Haha.

I've got one thing to say to Violet and Shawn— You shoulda brought a *towel*!

Hahahaha!

21

A deep shadow covered us as the hull of the big pirate ship rose, sending up tall waves. A frothy white-capped wave leaped high, then came sweeping forward.

I held on to Shawn with both hands. The wave crashed over our tiny raft, sending it toppling over. Shawn and I flew into the air. I opened my mouth to scream but no sound came out.

I smacked the surface of the water hard, then sank into the cold. My mouth was still open. I swallowed a mouthful and started to choke.

I forced myself to the surface, still coughing. I wiped water from my eyes and searched desperately for my brother. I saw the raft—empty now—being carried away on the waves.

And then I saw Shawn, paddling frantically, waves pushing him one way, then the other.

"Shawn—" I tried to call to him. But my throat was still clogged with salt-thick ocean water.

The pirate ship bobbed beside us now, and I

saw something fly off the deck. It floated up, then hit the water beside us.

It was a net. A wide fisherman's net. The opening spread in front of us, and Shawn and I dove into it.

A few seconds later, our traveling companions, Madeline and Salty and Pepper, joined us, thrashing their arms and legs, eager to be pulled up to safety.

The net lifted us out of the water. We bounced off one another, moaning and groaning, gasping in breaths of fresh air. "So this is what it's like to be a tuna fish," I said.

Shawn didn't smile. He was concentrating on staying on his hands and knees as the net rose higher and swung us onto the ship's deck.

We landed hard on the wooden planks. I landed on my side, and pain shot up and down my whole body. I breathed steadily, waiting for it to fade.

I wasn't about to complain. We were alive. Back onboard a ship. I thought we were safe.

I didn't know that we were still in horrible trouble.

22

The black sails rippled overhead and the ship rocked gently over the low waves. Sailors surrounded us. They pulled us out of the heavy rope net.

I know that it's not right to judge people by their looks. But these men were mean looking. Frightening. Tough. Their beards were long and their hair was wild. They had tattoos of anchors and mermaids over their arms. Their uniforms were stained and torn.

They spit and cursed as they dragged us out of the net and stood us in a line against the cabin wall. A tall redheaded pirate tugged my brother by the hair and tossed him in line.

Three or four of them circled Salty and Pepper and shoved back their heads, laughing. "Hey, mate, aren't you the pretty one?"

"Haha. Who says two heads are better than one? This one would look a lot better with *no* head."

"Maybe Captain Billy will do this guy a favor and cut them both off!"

"Where is my luggage?" Madeline demanded. "Did you take it to my first-class cabin?"

I could see she was back to her crazy act again.

"Thank you for rescuing us," I said, my voice coming out tiny and high.

"You'd best be saving your thank-yous," the red-haired pirate said, scowling. "Captain Billy Bottoms will have plans for you. And my guess is, you're not going to like them."

I heard heavy footsteps. We all turned and saw a large man striding toward us. He wore a bright yellow shirt, ruffled at the sleeves, under a purple jacket that came down to his knees. His trousers were purple, too.

He had long, shiny black hair, parted in the middle of his head and falling down to his shoulders. His eyes were round and dark, and he had a wire-thin mustache under his nose, curled up on both sides.

His face was fat and as round as a basketball. He was nearly as wide as he was tall. His body reminded me of a purple pumpkin with a head on top.

He was so weird looking, I almost laughed. But I held myself in when I saw his men stand at attention and grow silent. I could see they were afraid of him.

"Well, well," he said in a squeaky voice. "What

106

do we have here? What ugly seaweed has washed up from the waters below?" He rubbed his pudgy hands together.

"Our good old ship sank, Captain," Salty answered. "The *Jolly Sea Scab* went down yesterday. You heard of our ship, of course?"

"No," the captain said sharply. "Never heard of it. Never wanted to." He tugged at the ends of his wiry mustache.

I shoved back my drenched hair. "Thank you for rescuing us, Captain," I said.

He turned to me and studied me for a long moment. "Don't thank me yet, young miss. I haven't decided if you sea slugs are all worth keeping. Maybe I'll have to toss you back." He laughed.

"Welcome to my ship, the *Slimy Sea Worm.* I'm Captain Billy Bottoms, and I'm known as the Pimple of the South Seas. Do you know why I'm known as the Pimple of the South Seas?"

No one spoke. We all stared back at him. Finally, Madeline broke the silence: "Because people like to squeeze you?"

He squinted at her. "Are you crazy?"

She nodded. "That's what everyone tells me. How about you?"

Billy Bottoms's round face turned as purple as his suit. He narrowed his eyes at his men, who waited at attention across the deck. "I've decided what to do with these sea slugs," he said.

My heart skipped a beat. Would he really toss us back into the ocean?

Captain Billy rubbed his chubby hands together again. "I'm going to take them to the next island where they'll be held as prisoners."

Shawn and I both gasped. "But—but—" I sputtered.

He raised a hand to silence me. "Captain Billy Bottoms has made up his mind. You'll go to work in the banana fields. You'll enjoy it. All the bananas you can eat! Hahaha!"

He stepped up to me, his dark eyes wild. "Still want to thank me, Missy?"

"You—you can't *do* that!" I blurted out.

He laughed again. "I'm the Pimple of the South Seas. I can do whatever I please." He motioned to his men. "Take them down below."

But then he stopped. He narrowed his eyes at Salty and Pepper, as if seeing them for the first time. Bottoms rubbed his fat cheeks, thinking hard. "Hey," he said to the two-headed sailor, "Don't I know you? Haven't I seen you somewhere before?"

Salty and Pepper both nodded. "Yes, Captain Billy," Salty said. "We sailed together, you and I, on the *Sour Petunia*. Remember?"

Bottoms thought about it. "Oh, right. We were mates. Now I remember."

"Thank you for rescuing us," Pepper said.

"Since we were mates and sailed together, I guess you'll change your mind. You'll let us go."

Bottoms stroked his triple chins. "I just remembered something," he said. "I don't like you. I didn't like you *then*—and I don't like you now. In fact, I *hate* you both!"

"But I've changed a lot!" Salty cried. "Maybe you'll like me now. Maybe we'll be best friends forever."

"I don't think so," Bottoms said. He turned to the red-haired sailor. "Smitty, set our course for the island. And lock up the prisoners."

23

"I love a good banana when it's ripe," Madeline said.

Salty and Pepper stared at her. "Don't bananas grow on trees?" Salty asked. "That means we'll have to climb trees to pick them, and I'm afraid of heights."

"I'm afraid of *depths*," Pepper said. "I'd rather climb banana trees than be down at the bottom of the ocean."

Shawn and I mumbled agreement.

"I hate bananas," I said. "They're too sticky. They always get stuck on the roof of my mouth."

"You should try *chewing* them," Madeline said.

We were locked in a dark, smelly cabin at the bottom of the ship. We talked about bananas because what was *really* on our minds was too frightening.

But I couldn't keep my thoughts from going there . . .

I'm going to be a banana worker on a strange island.

Shawn and I will never get home. We'll never see our parents again.

It was much easier to talk about bananas than to talk about our real fears.

We all jumped in surprise when Smitty, the red-haired sailor, appeared carrying a tray of food bowls. "Help yourselves," he said. "The captain sent you some dinner."

I stared at the yellow mush in the bowls. "What is it?" I asked.

"Banana pudding," Smitty answered. He laughed. "Captain Billy Bottoms has an awesome sense of humor."

"Awesome," I muttered.

The next morning, Shawn and I were jolted as the ship bumped hard. I caught my balance as the cabin floor seemed to bounce. Then it came to rest, and I realized we had docked.

A short while later, Smitty appeared down below. He and the other pirates led us up to the deck. My knees ached and my legs were stiff from not moving.

As we stepped out of the hold, I raised my eyes to the sky. It was solid blue, and a bright yellow sun was already high above us. I took several deep breaths. It felt so good to get the stale air out of my lungs and some fresh sea air in.

"What is this island called?" Salty asked Smitty.

Smitty grinned at him. "It's called Your New Home."

The ship bobbed gently against the dock. Shawn peered over the deck and pointed. "You can see banana trees for miles!"

I followed his gaze. I saw a narrow sandy beach beyond the dock. I saw some men dressed in white shirts and shorts, wearing wide white hats. They had their eyes on the ship. They stood near a line of open horse-drawn carts, all filled to the top with mountains of bananas.

"I could go for a banana split," Madeline said.

Captain Billy Bottoms appeared and came bounding toward us. He had a wide grin on his red, round face. His shiny black hair caught the sunlight and made him glow as if he was on fire.

"Good morning, plantation workers," he said in his squeaky voice. "Your new home isn't far from here."

"Can we talk about this?" Salty asked. "Since we were old mates . . ."

"You're going to be a problem," Bottoms said, scowling at Salty. "There isn't much demand for a two-headed worker. You eat twice as much."

"I'm a good sailor, Captain," Salty insisted. "I could join your crew. It would be like old times."

"I *hate* the old times," Bottoms shouted. "And I hate you." He slapped the side of the deck. "Enough talk. Smitty, take them down to their new bosses."

Smitty saluted and motioned for us to follow him down the gangplank to the dock.

"Don't slip on any banana peels!" Bottoms cried. And then he laughed until his face was beet red and tears poured from his eyes.

We followed Smitty down to the island. We were about to start our new lives on a banana plantation.

In other words, we were doomed.

I felt a hand on my shoulder. I turned to find Madeline leaning close. She motioned to Shawn. "Listen, you two," she whispered. "I wasn't kidding about a banana split."

I blinked. "Huh? What do you mean?"

24

"When I give the signal, we split!" Madeline exclaimed.

"You mean run?" Shawn asked.

She nodded. "Duck under the banana carts and run to the fields on the other side."

My heart fluttered in my chest. "Okay," I whispered. "What's the signal?"

"Hey—no talking!" Smitty shouted. He stepped between us, his eyes darting angrily from Madeline to me. He grabbed each of us by the shoulder. "What were you talking about?"

"How handsome you look in that sailor uniform," Madeline replied.

He squinted at her. "You think so? I just had it washed six months ago. That's why it looks so sharp." Then he added with a grin, "You're going to love picking bananas."

"I'd rather pick my nose," Madeline said. She tossed back her head and laughed a long hoarse laugh.

The plantation owners heard Madeline's strange laugh and looked at us.

"Is she crazy?" one of them asked.

"Who? Mad Madeline?" Smitty said. "Of *course* she isn't crazy. She's just in a good mood because she loves bananas."

"Banana split," Madeline whispered. She gave Shawn and me a push, and we took off running. Our shoes thudded on the sand as we headed to the line of banana carts on the road. I glanced back and saw Salty and Pepper following us, taking long, running strides.

"They're getting away!" a sailor shouted from behind us.

"Stop them! Get them!"

Smitty and the other sailors were close behind. The plantation owners came running, shouting and waving their arms.

They're too fast, I realized. *We'll never escape. Where can we run?*

Madeline ducked her head and dove under a banana cart. Shawn and I and Salty and Pepper followed, diving under the cart, then crawling to the other side.

The carts were lined up all down the narrow dirt road that led away from the beach. The horses pulling the carts all stood very still with their heads down. The open cart beds were bulging with bananas. The banana fields started on this side of the road and seemed to stretch for miles.

The shouts of the men grew louder. I could hear their running footsteps on the other side of the carts.

I struggled to catch my breath as we ran. "Where can we go?" I called to Madeline a few feet ahead of us. "If we run into the fields, they'll catch us. We can't run down the road. They'll catch us there, too."

Madeline pointed to the back of a cart. "Maybe we can hide."

Hide in the bananas? It didn't seem to make sense. But we didn't have time to discuss it.

Madeline scrambled onto the back of a cart. I gave Shawn a boost. Then I pulled myself up after him. Salty and Pepper burst in right behind us.

"Get under the bananas," Madeline said breathlessly. "Hurry. It's our only chance."

The four of us began frantically lifting up bunches of bananas, trying to slide under them. I saw Madeline and Salty and Pepper disappear under blankets of the green fruit.

Shawn was having trouble with the heavy bunches. I turned and swung a long bunch over his chest. I could hear the men getting closer, hear their running footsteps on the dirt road.

No time. No time.

I covered Shawn's face with another bunch. Then I dropped onto my back, desperately grabbing at bananas, pulling them over me.

The sweet smell of the just-picked bananas invaded my nose. My stomach lurched. The aroma was making me sick. I held my breath and forced my stomach to stop heaving.

I heard the shouts of the men. They had to be just *inches* away from us.

I ducked as low as I could, pressing myself against the flat bed of the cart. I couldn't see a thing, not even a glimpse of sunlight. I hoped the bananas covered me. I couldn't tell.

Was Shawn completely covered, too? I couldn't see him. But I could hear his wheezing breaths close beside me.

I held my breath. My skin started to itch. I struggled not to move.

And then a powerful hand gripped my leg.

25

Caught.

I opened my mouth to scream, but no sound came out.

It took me a few seconds to realize it was Shawn's hand. The poor frightened guy held on to my leg.

Over my thundering heartbeats, I heard voices outside the cart.

"Where did they go?" a man shouted, inches away.

"Into the field?"

"Did they go back to the dock?"

"They can't get back on the ship. Bottoms has his men posted on the lookout for them."

"They didn't go far. Keep searching!"

Under the heavy bananas, I flattened myself against the cart bed and listened for them to move away. My skin was itching like crazy now. But I forced myself not to move a muscle.

I heard the soft thud of footsteps on the sandy ground as the men moved past the carts. Their voices grew fainter. I was still afraid to move. Had any of them lingered nearby?

I waited and listened. And then I felt something warm crawling over the back of my neck. Like soft pinpricks. The touch made my skin tingle.

And then I felt another one, in my hair. Hard pinprick legs scuttling over the top of my head.

Bugs? Bugs in the bananas?

I couldn't help it. I jerked myself up, knocking bunches of bananas to the side. I grabbed at the back of my neck. Wrapped my fingers around something soft and spindly.

Raised it to my horrified face. And started to scream.

"Tarantulas!"

I felt the soft tickle of one crawling up my right leg. Frantically, I slapped at my hair—and a tarantula came toppling out. It scrabbled away on its slender legs, under the bunches of bananas.

Had anyone seen me sit up? Had the men heard my scream?

Pushing a heavy bunch of bananas off my lap, I gazed around. I could see the men deep in the field, searching for us among the clusters of banana trees.

Shawn sat up, eyes wide with fright. He gasped in a few deep breaths. Sweat poured down his face.

I reached over and tugged at a tarantula on the front of his T-shirt. It clung to his shirt. It didn't want to come off. But I swung it away and tossed it across the cart bed.

Salty and Pepper shoved bananas off them. "They won't bite unless they're hungry," Salty said.

"Yes, they will," Pepper argued.

Madeline's head popped up from a bunch of bananas. "I . . . I hate tarantulas," she said. "I—I—Eeeewwww!" She shook her whole body, like a dog shaking off water.

My skin itched and tingled. "We have to get out of here," I said. "Look!" I pointed.

The men had turned around. They were trotting back toward the carts.

"Where can we go?" Shawn demanded. "We—we're trapped here."

Before anyone could answer, the cart lurched hard. It shot backward, then jerked forward. I bounced into Shawn, and we both flew into the back of the cart bed.

The banana bunches bounced with us, and I saw tarantulas topple off the fruit and scurry across the cart bed.

"Whoa—wait! We're moving!" I cried as the horse groaned loudly, then pulled the cart into the center of the dirt road.

We began rumbling over the road, picking up speed.

I turned to my brother, my eyes wide with fear. "Wh-where is it taking us?" I cried.

26

The four of us bounced in the back of the cart as it sped along the dirt road. Every bump sent us flying. Shawn and I gripped banana bunches with both hands to help hold us down and keep us from flying over the side.

The cart followed a curve into the middle of a banana tree field. The thick bunches of green bananas bumped the sides of the cart as we sped past.

"I think we should jump out," Salty shouted over the roar of the cart.

"No, we shouldn't," Pepper said.

"If we stay in the cart, we'll be caught," Salty warned.

"If we jump, we'll break our necks," his other head insisted.

They were still arguing about what to do when the cart squealed to a stop. All four of us slammed into the side. Pain shot up my back. Shawn struggled to climb to his feet.

I gazed around. We had stopped in a tiny village. I saw a row of white shacks. An old carriage with a missing wheel stood in front of a little store. Two kids eating popcorn leaned in the doorway to a shop.

"Hurry. Move!" Salty shouted. "We're out of here!"

He leaped out of the back of the cart. Brushed a tarantula off his shoulder. Turned and ran toward the small store.

Shawn and I helped Madeline off the cart. Then the three of us started to run. We heard the cart driver shout behind us. "Stop! Hey—stop, you!" But we didn't look back and we didn't stop.

My heart was pounding as we followed Salty and Pepper along the side of the little store to the back. I heard music coming from inside. Soft classical music, the kind my parents like.

Salty and Pepper had stopped to talk to two girls about my age. They were sitting on a railing, books in their hands.

I stopped and stared at them. They were both blond, both tall, wearing long skirts and ruffled white blouses.

Shawn, Madeline, and I stepped up beside Salty. The girls squinted at us, shielding their eyes from the sun with their hands. "Where did *you* come from?" one of them asked.

"It's a long story," I said. "Where are we?"

They both laughed. "You don't know where you are?"

"We were kind of kidnapped," Shawn said.

The girls stopped laughing. "Why do you look so frightened? Are you in trouble? Are people coming after you? We don't want any trouble." They jumped down from the railing and started to hurry away.

"No, please—" Salty called after them. "Just tell us what island this is."

"Is this Banana Island?" Pepper asked.

The girls laughed again. "Banana Island? No way!"

"It was a good guess," Pepper said.

"This isn't Banana Island," one of them said. "It's Clam Island."

"Huh?" I gasped. The others reacted in surprise. "Clam Island? But it's all bananas. Why is it called Clam Island?"

"Because the island is shaped like a clamshell," a girl said.

"Clam Island!" I exclaimed. "That's just where we want to be!"

"Well, you made it," one of them said. "Good luck." And they hurried away, disappearing around the corner of the little store.

Salty and Pepper slapped their foreheads. "Do you believe it? Captain Billy dropped us off exactly where we were supposed to go," Salty said. "How lucky is that?"

"And there is something even *luckier*," Pepper said. "Look. You won't believe it." He pointed to a low bush.

Perched on the top branch of the bush was a yellow canary.

I gasped. This was impossible. Could we *really* be this lucky? If we returned the canary to Jack the Knife, my uncle Jim would be safe, and the pirates would all go back in their boxes. Our lives could return to normal.

I was nearly bursting with excitement. "Wh-what does Captain Jack's canary look like?" I whispered.

"It has a pip on its forehead," Salty whispered back. "That's why he's named Captain Pip."

We crept on tiptoe closer to the bush. I held my breath. Would we scare it away?

"What does a pip look like?" Shawn whispered.

I shrugged. "I don't know."

"See that dot on his forehead?" Pepper said. "That's a pip. That's him, all right."

Madeline and Salty held back, eyes locked on the canary. I took another step closer . . . Another . . .

And in the fastest move I ever made in my life, I shot my hand forward, gently grabbed the canary, and wrapped my fingers around it.

"Got it!" I cried. "Look! I got Captain Pip!"

I spun around and raised my hand to show it to the others. Pip cheeped once—and flew out of my hand.

The four of us watched in silence as the canary fluttered out of sight.

27

"I don't *believe* it!" I cried. "I had him. I really had him." I tightened my hands into fists and pumped the air angrily.

"I guess it was too good to be true," Shawn said.

Madeline stepped up to us. "No worries," she said. "Watch."

She sat down on the sandy ground and crossed her arms in front of her. Then she tilted her head to the sky, and began to go "tweet tweet tweet" in a high bird voice.

The rest of us stared down at her, our mouths open.

"Tweet tweet tweettweet tweettweet chirp-chirp."

"I think she's gone crazy again," Shawn whispered to me.

"I heard that," Madeline said. "I'm not crazy. How do you think you get a canary to come back? By making canary sounds."

She turned away from us and began chirping and tweeting again.

Shawn and I exchanged glances. Did she really know how to call a canary back?

We didn't have to wait long to find out. Madeline was chirping her head off when the canary appeared. It fluttered over her for a few seconds. Then it sailed right into her open hand.

"Captain Pip, we've got you!" she cried happily. The rest of us cheered. She cupped the bird carefully in her hands.

We had come to Clam Island. We had captured Captain Jack's canary without hardly trying. We all agreed we had been *very* lucky.

But would our luck continue?

The answer was definitely *yes*. We found a little wooden birdcage in the village store that we could carry Captain Pip in. Lucky.

Then we walked back to the ocean through the banana tree fields. When we got to the dock, Captain Billy Bottoms's pirate ship was still there. Very lucky.

We crept on board and quickly discovered that the ship was *empty*. That's because Captain Billy and all his men were on Clam Island searching for us. The four of us lifted anchor and we set sail in Captain Billy's ship. Very, very lucky.

Salty and Pepper found a map in the captain's cabin, and we followed it on a calm sea right back to Sea Urchin Cove, Uncle Jim's town.

Luck, luck, and more luck.

By the time we climbed off the ship at the little dock in front of Uncle Jim's house we were very happy. In fact, Shawn and I were so happy, we did a crazy dance on the beach, flinging our arms in the air and shouting at the top of our lungs.

I've never been more happy or more excited, and I could see that Shawn felt the same way.

Of course, as we carried the cage with Captain Pip to the gray house over the shore, we knew we still had to face Jack the Knife.

And that's when our luck ran out.

He was waiting in the front room when the four of us came bursting in. We were all excited, all talking at once.

I saw Celeste, sitting up against the wall, her green eyes wide with surprise. The other pirates were all there. And their empty jack-in-the-boxes were still scattered over the floor.

Captain Jack raised his hook to silence us. He squinted at the wooden cage. "Well, I see ye all made it back," he said. "What have ye brought me?"

"Here he is, Captain Jack," I said, handing him the cage. "We did what you asked. We brought back your canary."

Jack took the cage from me with his good hand and raised it in front of his face. He brought it close and studied the bird for a long moment.

Then he turned to me with a low growl. "Sorry. That's not Captain Pip," he said.

28

I gasped. A heavy feeling of dread swept over me. My knees started to fold. "Oh no, oh no," I murmured.

"Ye failed," Jack said, lowering the birdcage to his side. "Captain Pip has a pip on his forehead. This canary doesn't have the pip."

"But—but—" I sputtered. I pointed into the cage. "What's that on the canary's head?"

"It's a pip," Jack replied. "But it's not the *right* pip."

Against the wall, Celeste raised her head. "Too bad," she murmured in her scratchy cat voice.

I saw Shawn's shoulders heave up and down. He was about to start crying. Madeline lowered her head and gazed at the floor. Salty and Pepper remained silent.

"Wrong canary," Jack repeated. "But that's no problem. This canary will do fine." He raised the cage to his face. "Pretty bird. Pretty bird."

"Huh? What did you just say?" I cried. "You'll take this canary?"

"Sure enough." He shrugged. "A canary is a canary. Who *cares* which one it is?" He poked a finger into the cage and tickled the bird's bill.

I wanted to jump for joy. I saw a big grin spread over my brother's face. "Yaaaay!" Shawn and I both burst out cheering.

"Does this mean you will keep your promise?" I demanded. "You will return our uncle Jim? And all of you pirates will go back in your jack-in-the-boxes?"

Captain Jack set down the birdcage. He lifted a square box off the floor. He turned the crank.

Shawn and I stared as Uncle Jim sprang up from the box. Jim's tiny hands bounced at his sides. His mouth hung open. His face was locked in an expression of horror.

"If ye ask me," Jack growled, "old Admiral Jim looks good right where he is. I think I'm going to leave him in his box."

He tossed back his head and laughed. It sounded like his throat was filled with gravel.

"But you *promised*!" Shawn cried. "You promised if we brought you the canary—"

Jack picked up Celeste and cradled the cat in one arm. "I *know* what I promised, young fella," he said. "But that was a *pirate's* promise. Do you know what a pirate's promise is worth?"

"What?" Shawn said.

"Nothing," Jack told him. "It's worthless. I made a pirate's promise. And a good pirate—like me—*never keeps a promise*!" He laughed his gravelly laugh again.

"How sad," Celeste said, lifting her head from Jack's arm.

I let out a long sigh. That whole terrifying trip we made was all for nothing.

"Tell ye what I *will* do," Jack said, a grin lingering on his face. "I'll turn ye and your brother into jack-in-the-boxes so ye can join your uncle. How's *that* for a deal?"

Jack started to laugh again, and all his pirates joined in.

He began to twirl his hook slowly in front of Shawn and me. And the room began to spin.

29

I gazed at the twirling hook in front of my face as it moved faster and faster in a small circle. I couldn't take my eyes off it. My body started to feel strange, as if it was beginning to shrink. And I couldn't do anything to stop it. Shawn and I would soon be trapped in boxes, too.

Then—suddenly—the hook stopped moving.

The room came back into focus. I blinked away my dizziness. And I saw that Jack and all the pirates were staring wide-eyed and open-mouthed at the wall.

Shawn and I turned and followed their gaze.

A cry escaped my throat as I saw an arm poking through the wall from outside. A bony arm wrapped in a torn shirtsleeve.

"What on earth—!" I murmured.

The arm poked straight through the wall, followed by a shoulder, then a man's chest. And as we all stared in silent shock, a man slid into the room.

But not a real man. Not a solid man. He appeared to be made of smoke. I could see right through him!

He stopped in front of the wall and stared around the room. His shirt and trousers were tattered, nearly in shreds. His eyes were wide and unblinking. They were solid white, like two eggshells. His beard was tangled and knotted. His long, patchy hair fell to the sides of his face.

I realized I was holding my breath. As the man took a step forward, I could see that some of the skin was missing on his forehead. I could see a square of his gray skull underneath.

He was drenched from head to toe, and his clothes dripped water onto the floor. Slowly, he raised a bony finger and pointed it at Captain Jack.

"Wh-who *are* you?" Jack demanded, squeezing Celeste in his arms.

It took the man a long time to answer. His mouth moved up and down, but no words came out at first. Water dribbled out over his tongue.

"I am Danny Lubbins," he said finally, his voice a terrifying whisper, like crackling leaves. "I am Danny Lubbins. Three hundred days at sea, and never made it to shore. But I'm here at last. Here at last."

Celeste's eyes went wide. She tilted her head, suddenly alert.

"Give me my cat!" the ghost cried, shaking a

bony finger at Captain Jack. "Give me my cat—or I'll take all of you to the grave with me!"

Captain Jack's eyes bulged in terror. He dropped Celeste to the floor. His whole body shook as he pointed his hook. "You—you're a *ghost?*"

The ghost nodded. More water rolled out from his mouth. "I'm the ghost of Danny Lubbins, and I've come for my cat."

Captain Jack went pale. His shoulders slumped. His body started to collapse. "I . . . I'm afraid of ghosts," he murmured. "And I'm afraid of the grave."

That's when the room went crazy. The pirates began to scream and slink back. Captain Jack backed up, his mouth open, frozen in horror. He stumbled over a box and fell to the floor.

The pirates' screams rang off the low ceiling. I watched in amazement as Jack and the pirates all grabbed boxes off the floor. In their terror, they began to shrink. It took only a few seconds.

Shawn and I stood with our mouths open as the tiny pirates jumped back into their jack-in-the-boxes and slammed the lids shut after them.

The room was suddenly silent.

I pressed my hands to my cheeks and stared in disbelief. The pirates were gone. One box stood by itself against the back wall. It popped open—and the puppet-sized Uncle Jim sprang up.

"Oh, wow!" I cried.

Uncle Jim grew quickly until he regained his normal size. He blinked several times, shaking his head, dazed. Then he hurried over to us.

And then the three of us watched as Celeste jumped into the ghost's arms. "Good-bye and thanks," she called in her scratchy voice. And the ghost of Danny Lubbins disappeared back into the wall and vanished with the cat.

It was all too much, too frightening, too crazy. I struggled to catch my breath.

"Well, well. A busy day," Uncle Jim said. He squinted at Shawn and me. "How are you kids doing? Sorry I didn't check in sooner. Don't know where the day went! Hope you weren't bored."

SLAPPY HERE.

Uncle Jim seems a little out of it, if you ask me. Where has he been living—in a *box*? Hahaha.

Do you know the best thing about being a jack-in-the-box? It's always *spring*time! Haha. Get it?

That's one of Slappy's little jokes.

Jack the Knife and I have a lot in common. For one thing, we both like canaries. Only I like mine *cooked* and served on rice! Hahaha!

Well, don't worry, slaves. I'll be back soon with another Goosebumps story.

Remember, this is Slappy's world.

You only *scream* in it!

They walk alike, they talk alike, they scream alike!

I AM SLAPPY'S EVIL TWIN

Here's a sneak peek!

1

Franz Mahar strokes his white beard and gazes down at the face of the puppet he is making. The glassy olive-green eyes stare up at him. The doll's wooden face is still unpainted. The smooth lips are frozen in a pale grin.

From the open window of his workshop, Mahar hears the bleating of sheep. The farmers of the small village herd their flocks to the high pasture every morning. Then they bring the animals down as the afternoon sun begins to lower itself over the sloping hills.

The village stands eighty miles from the nearest large town. Nothing has changed in a hundred years. Cows and goats and pigs roam free. Mahar awakes to the sound of clucking chickens every morning.

Mahar raises a long needle and leans over the worktable. He begins sewing cuffs on the puppet's stiff white shirt. His fingers tremble.

He is an old man now, with failing eyesight

and unsteady hands. Once he had been a star of the London stage. He had created a ventriloquist dummy so lifelike, audiences were amazed. They filled theaters to see his act. He had fame and enough money to enjoy it.

But then, there had been trouble. He shared the stage with the magician Kanduu. With his swirling scarlet cape and his ability to make *anything* appear or disappear, Kanduu was also a star.

They became friends. Mahar trusted Kanduu. He didn't realize—until too late—that Kanduu's magic came from a dark place. Kanduu was a sorcerer.

He could cast spells, and his spells were always evil. He could control people. He could make them say and do things they didn't want to do.

Mahar learned a lot of magic from Kanduu. He didn't realize that Kanduu had an evil side. Until one day backstage when Mahar was about to begin his act.

He opened the long black case in which he kept Mr. Wood, his dummy. He bent down and began to lift the dummy from the case.

"Oww!" Mahar cried out as the dummy's wooden hand swung up and punched him hard in the chin.

"Keep your hands off me!" Mr. Wood shouted. Mahar stood there, staring in shock at him, rubbing the pain from his jaw.

"*I'm pulling the strings from now on!*" the dummy declared. He swung his wooden fist again and caught Mahar on the shoulder.

Backing away, Mahar realized what had happened. Kanduu had enchanted the dummy. Kanduu had poured his evil magic into Mahar's creation. Mr. Wood was *alive*.

Terrified, Mahar slammed the case shut. He left it on the stage. He never wanted to see that dummy again. He packed a bag and sailed for the United States.

Mahar was desperate to flee, to leave the evil dummy behind. He hid away in this tiny farm village and built a small cottage and a workshop. He lived quietly, alone. He made no friends.

He *built* his only friends. The puppets and dolls he created in his workshop were works of art. His hands gently carved their wooden heads and hands. He painted their faces. He sewed their costumes.

He gave them personalities. He did puppet shows and ventriloquist acts for himself. And once in a while, he used the magic he had learned from Kanduu. Some nights, he brought his puppets and dummies to life. He did it out of loneliness. He needed someone to talk to.

So today—while the sheep bleat and the chickens cluck outside his window—Mahar puts the final touches on his latest creation.

He finishes coloring the dummy's cheeks with gentle strokes of a small brush.

"You are made from the finest hardwood," he tells the dummy. "And I have used the powers I learned to give you life."

On its back on the worktable, the dummy blinks its glassy eyes.

"You will obey me at all times," Mahar says, pulling it up to a sitting position. He ties the dummy's polished brown shoes.

"The magic I have poured into you can be dangerous. You must stay under my control. You must not follow any angry or cruel thoughts."

The dummy blinks again. Does it understand Mahar's words?

Mahar has more instructions for his creation. But he is interrupted by a knocking on the wooden cottage door.

He jumps in surprise. "Who is pounding on my door so violently?"

It sounds like more than one fist beating at the door, hard enough to break it open.

"I'm coming. I'm coming," Mahar murmurs. He sets the dummy onto its back on the worktable.

Then he wipes his aged hands on the sides of his overalls and limps to the door. He pulls it open slowly—and utters a loud gasp.

The entire village?

Mahar's eyes blur as he sweeps his gaze over

the grim-faced men and women. At least two dozen of them. His legs begin to tremble. He tries to focus. Some of them carry torches. The men standing at the front of the group carry pistols.

Mahar feels his throat tighten. He begins to choke.

Finally, he finds his voice. "What do you want? Why are you here? What are you going to do?"

2

They all begin to shout at once. They shake angry fists at him. The flames from the torches shoot forward, as if attacking him. Men raise their pistols high in warning.

"Please—" Mahar begs. "Please—"

Two farmers in overalls lower their shoulders and push Mahar back from the doorway. He stumbles against the wall. Shouting and cursing, the villagers burst into his cottage.

They fill his front room. They wave the flaming torches angrily. A flower vase crashes to the floor. In the roar of voices, Mahar struggles to hear their words.

"Please explain—" he begs.

The two farmers step up to him. They are big men, tall with big bellies behind their overalls. Mud clings to the cuffs of their pants. One is bald, the other has shaggy blond hair that falls around his face. Their red foreheads are dripping with sweat.

146

"I am Buster Bailey," the bald one declares. "My neighbor here is Seth Johnson. I believe you've seen us in the village."

Mahar nods.

They narrow their eyes at him. "You know what you have done," Bailey growls.

"N-no," Mahar stammers. "I . . . I have done nothing."

"It is you who has brought the bad luck to our village," the farmer says through clenched jaws.

"Yes, it is you," Johnson repeats, shaking a meaty fist. "Our village is in ruins. The crops have withered and died."

"But—but—" Mahar sputters.

Johnson raises his hand to silence him. "The cows are all giving sour milk."

"Yesterday, a two-headed goat was born on my farm," Bailey growls. "The evil spreads from day to day. And *you* are the one who has brought it to us."

His words make the crowd of villagers begin to shout out their anger. Mahar sees some of them raise fists. They move forward, ready to attack.

He tries to protest. But their shouts drown out his words.

"It's the dolls!" a woman cries. Her face is red and angry beneath a long gray scarf. "Look! There's a new one!"

They turn to the dummy on its back on the worktable.

"The doll! It's the doll!"

"Destroy it!"

"The doll is evil. Look at that evil face."

Bailey grabs Mahar by the front of his work shirt. "Your dolls have brought a dozen misfortunes to our village."

"N-no—" Mahar stammers. "No. You are wrong. They are just dolls, made of wood and cloth."

"Evil! Evil! Evil!" Some villagers begin the chant.

All eyes are on Mahar's dummy. The villagers' faces are twisted in fear.

"Evil! Kill the evil! Kill the evil!"

Bailey shoves Mahar aside and strides to the workbench.

"No!" Mahar screams. But he is helpless to stop them.

The farmer grabs the dummy by its waist and hoists it over his head.

The shouts stop suddenly. A hush falls over the cottage. The dummy's arms and legs hang limply from Bailey's meaty hand. Its head is tilted back. Its eyes gaze glassily to the ceiling.

"Please—" Mahar begs. "The doll is my life's work! It took years to make. I beg you—"

The farmer lowers his shoulder and shoves Mahar out of the way again. Mahar stumbles back against the worktable. The two farmers start toward the door. The crowd steps back to allow them room to leave.

"Burn it!" someone shouts.

"Burn the doll!" cries the woman in the gray scarf.

"Burn it! Burn it!"

The farmers lumber out of the cottage. Bailey still holds the dummy high over his head.

His heart pounding, Mahar watches from the doorway of his cottage as the villagers work together to build a bonfire. His whole body trembles, and he feels as if his heart may burst open.

The smell of their fear lingers in his cottage. He can't erase their angry faces from his mind. Such hatred and superstition. How could these people suspect an innocent doll of bringing bad luck to their village?

The villagers work in silence. They stack tree branches and sticks of kindling in a high pile on the dirt road across from Mahar's cottage.

They scatter dead, dry leaves at the bottom to make the fire catch quickly. It doesn't take long to build a tall mountain of wood.

In the distance, Mahar hears the sad bleating of goats in their pasture. He tries to picture the two-headed goat.

He is still picturing it as the torches are lowered to the woodpile. The flames catch quickly. Mahar holds his breath and watches the fire climb the mound of sticks and branches.

When the flames have reached the top, the fire crackles and snaps. The yellow-orange flames dance and leap about.

The villagers have formed a circle around the bonfire. Mahar watches their eager faces, lighted by the fire. Their eyes are wide with excitement. The only sound is the crackling of leaves and sticks.

Johnson, his long blond hair glowing from the fire, breaks the silence with a booming shout. *"Good-bye to evil!"*

"Good-bye to evil!" villagers shout.

"Good-bye to evil! Good-bye to evil!"

Mahar gasps as Bailey heaves the dummy into the flames. The fire surrounds the dummy. Its suit jacket and pants erupt in flames.

And then, as Mahar watches from the cottage doorway, the fire swallows the dummy. It disappears into the swirling flames as if being eaten in one gulp.

And from behind the dancing, darting flames, a *howl* of pain and horror rings out over the crowd of silent onlookers.

About the Author

R.L. Stine's books are read all over the world. So far, his books have sold more than 300 million copies, making him one of the most popular children's authors in history. Besides Goosebumps, R.L. Stine has written the teen series Fear Street and the funny series Rotten School, as well as the Mostly Ghostly series, The Nightmare Room series, and the two-book thriller *Dangerous Girls*. R.L. Stine lives in New York with his wife, Jane, and Minnie, his King Charles spaniel. You can learn more about him at www.RLStine.com.